Sunshine
and
Rays of Hope

by

James Benedict

DORRANCE
PUBLISHING CO
EST. 1920
PITTSBURGH, PENNSYLVANIA 15238

Dorrance Publishing Co.
585 Alpha Drive
Suite 103
Pittsburgh, PA 15238
Visit our website at *www.dorrancebookstore.com*

ISBN: 978-1-4809-4636-1
eISBN: 978-1-4809-4613-2

Contents

Chapter 1
The Struggles of Life

Top of the morning, do today what you may, for tomorrow is not a given. And just what should we be doing, you may ask? Do right, love goodness, and walk humbly with your God for there are three attributes in life that we should hold dear in our hearts. These are reverence for God, respect for life and honor to do what is right.

Life is a special gift, an endowment that destines each of us to glorify beyond all bounds God's marvelous bounty. But life is not so fortuitous for each person due to war, disease or strife, whether it is political, religious, social or economic and the struggles force us to gaze through the clouds of despair for the sunshine and rays of hope. Throughout the millennia, many civilizations have disappeared; great cultures have existed and melting pots arose to forge a new, stronger, resilient people. From these cultures, America, land of the so-called brave, arose from the tumultuous past of many lands. Yes, life is a gift, but we were never promised that it would be easy.

As everywhere in Europe, the seventeenth century marks a turning point for the powers in charge. Continual warfare dominates the region throughout the seventeenth and eighteenth centuries, and by the 1850s poverty, emigration and depopulation weaken Scandinavia and other nations while the Russian empire continues to prosper, dominating Europe and becoming a major player in world affairs. Over a million Swedes left their homeland between 1850 and 1900, most of them settling in the United States.

And this is where our story begins with two very distinctive nationalities, two different struggles, and two very pretentious sets of brothers. Svante and Lucas were born during upheaval years in the old country of Sweden in the county of Gavleborg, just due north of Stockholm as the Kestrel flies. Large numbers of seabirds of several species, such as guillemots, kittiwakes and shags, could be seen along the shores of the Gavle River as merchant ships made their way to the town of Gavle. Gavle is a city with a proud tradition of shipbuilding, and during the 1800s, there were several major shipyards that built merchant sailing ships. The boy's dad, who was a merchant mariner, just like his own dad, had sailed the seven seas and wished for a prosperous, good life for his sons. But, as fate would have it, times were a struggle since the outbreak of the Napoleonic Wars, and Sweden, which was once a great power, now was only a second-rate nation in the conflict of European power politics. Gustavus Bergstrom Sr. served with distinction in the third Napoleonic War during the march from Pomerania to the Netherlands. It was a disastrous war where Gustavus Sr. was fatally shot and never received any military glory but faded in time from the memories of that campaign. The only ones that kept his memory alive were his family, especially Gustavus Jr., who now only thought about a future for his boys. He helped raise his three younger brothers with his surviving, aging mother and encouraged them to finish school and later work in the shipyards. Now, a few years later and hopefully a few years wiser, he encouraged his own sons to become apprentices in the ship building trade and hopefully a more stable life then traveling on the seven seas. The sons, now eighteen and sixteen respectively, were as different as day and night. Svante was reticent, calculative, and introverted due to the harsh upbringing by his dad who taught him the three R's of life. Respect, rationalization, and being retrospective were not only ideals highly held by the dad but were the principles that Gustavus instilled into his sons as they had grown up. No disrespect was tolerated, and if one should talk back, then all hell broke loose as the belt was quickly retrieved and three lashings were given. Svante, being the oldest, bore most of the harsh discipline, whereas Lucas learned what not to do by observing his brother's follies. Gustavus Bergstrom was raised on the sea and now commanded his own ship as captain and knew far too well what an undisciplined individual could do. Lashings and keelhauling were a part of life at sea; it was not that he didn't love his sons, but he understood all too well what it meant to be the master of his ship and home. Lucas was always protected and under the wings of his older brother. He grew as a gregarious, blithesome young lad full of hell and enjoyed life and all its challenges. Under the tutelage of their father they learned and enjoyed the three S's: sailing, skiing, and service, for Gustavus believed in service to God, country, and family. The one event that brought them close together without any indifference was their zeal for sailing. Sails to the wind were their passion and shear enjoyment of being together.

But as fate always finds a way to carve and shape a new path of destiny, the economic strife that descended upon Sweden like a cannon ball devastated the economic times of the country. And to add insult to injury during those times when Russia acquired Finland in 1809, there was an influx of Fins to Sweden that caused competitive attitudes for land, jobs, and economic despair. In Gavle five of the seven shipyards closed due to competitive bids from foreign competition. Even in the 1800s it was beginning to be a cut-throat, global market. The dominance of the great landowners and the strife of economic decadence of the times would force many to choose a better way of life. God willing, there had to be a better way of life!

Across the Baltic Sea in a foreign land, a different sort of struggle was forming and would influence many to also choose a better way of life. Otto was a man of principles and raised in the Roman, Catholic faith. He grew up and was educated in the local parochial schools of Witzen-hausen, a lively city in the beautiful landscape valley of the river Werra right in the heart of Prussia. Centuries of tumultuous wars from various Teutonic and Slavic tribes molded cultures and civilizations or destroyed them like the Roman Empire and forged what came to be Germany. Constant upheaval can cause pandemonium throughout the centuries and divided convictions of credence that can lead many down a wrong path in life. During the 1200s Prussia was conquered by the Teutonic Knights, a military religious order, who converted or forced the Prussians to Christianity. Within the next two hundred years, the Teutonic Knights were overthrown by the Prussians with the aid and cunning persistence from Poland and Lithuania in the 1400s. Once upheaval begins it never stops, for the 1500s ushered in the Protestant Reformation and saw most Prussians converted to Protestantism. Beliefs are good if they are sincerely embraced within our heat, conscience and soul of God, but history has failed us with too much disturbance and war, causing many hearts to be hardened and turn from the One that gave us the gift of life.

Culture struggles have always been difficult but there was one that erupted within Prussia known as the "Kulturkampf,"

German policies about the secularity and abolishing the role of the Roman Catholic Church in the homeland. Priests and bishops who resisted the Kulturkampf were arrested or removed from their positions. During this tenacious period, most of the bishops were put in prison, parishes had no priest, half of the monks and nuns had left Prussia, hundreds of parish priests were imprisoned along with thousands of laypeople who helped the clergy.

Now Otto, who had just returned from Rome completing his studies for the priesthood, was to be ordained and assigned to a local parish in his hometown of Witzenhausen. His ordination would be a testimony to God who called him forth and his parents who raised him well within the faith. He had fond memories of his adolescent years of fishing, hunting and woodworking that he learned from his dad who taught all his children including the girls. Otto couldn't help but chuckle to himself as flashbacks of winter enjoyment on those snowbound slops with his sisters and brothers. Rosy cheeks, red noses, and their strickmutzes, knitted caps, pulled down over their ears as their toboggan cruised down the slopes. Returning under a cloud of despair and finding his dad arrested for helping the local parish, Otto was in complete dismay. His grossvater, formal for father, Dietrich Zimmermann was a kind hearted and generous man. Humble in his trade as a carpenter, he had made the new altar for the local church and spent many hours carving the oak timbers with elegant craftsmanship. He also made with pride two toboggans that could seat twelve so that the entire family, including Mama and Papa, could enjoy the ride. What should have been a joyous return was now an agonizing nightmare of terror.

Axel, his older brother, met Otto at the train depot and embraced his brother in tears.

"I'm afraid Otto these are dreadful times and a sad reunion indeed!" Axel told his brother.

"Papa has been arrested, along with your brothers, Ludwig and Bernhard, and I'm afraid that Mater has taken ill with all that has transpired."

Otto had to sit down on a bench for he could not fathom all that his brother was trying to tell him. How could these changes take place in the last six years from the time that he had left his home town of Witzenhausen?

The Zimmermann family was a large, congenial clan of some twenty-two children and felt so well blessed that they adopted two more to add to the flock. Otto was the third from the youngest of twelve boys and ten sisters. Hearty stock that felt life was a blessing and indeed lived life to the fullest. The older children raised the younger ones as each one took a younger one under their wings sort to speak. Otto remembered being seated in front of his brother on the toboggan with Axel's protective arms holding him in securely. The evenings were spent around the camp fire with warm cider and the singing of Johann Sebastian

Bach's cantatas, one of the greatest composers of Germany for Christian worship which inspired Otto to contemplate the priesthood. Now as Axel tried to warn Otto that he would be arrested if he didn't disappear, he handed him a letter from their dad. The letter read:

Otto,

You must take your two younger brothers, Kurt & Wolfgang, and escape to America as soon as possible, for there is no future here for our faith. God is love and His laws are for our good and not a burden as many people here believe, but a delightful way of life that ultimately produces the good things we really want in life – loving relationships, peace and real joy! Your older brothers & sisters will take care of Mater. As for me, my life is in God's hands.

God Speed.
Your loving Dad,
Dietrich

The tears were streaming down Otto's face as he embraced his brother, not knowing what to do next. But Axel and Stefan, one of his other brothers, had a plan all worked out.

Meanwhile back in Gavle, the Halva shipyard which was in strong competition with the Gotaverken shipyard was fighting to stay afloat and in business. Meeting time schedules and staying within budget was difficult enough but impromptu accidents were costly both in manpower and the Swedish riksdaler, their dollar. It was a race for the surviving shipyards to meet harsh demands for a triple mast schooner. Speed was of the essence to make port of calls faster than their competitors. And Hjalmar, proprietor of the shipyard who had sailed as captain on one of the three ships that he owned, had devised an ingenious device to expedite production. He devised a derrick, or hoisting apparatus of a tackle rigged at the end of a beam, and had successfully utilized the derrick to lower two masts in place at the same time. With a larger spreader-bar could they possibly engineer the derrick to lower three masts in place simultaneously? This indeed would push them ahead in the race to complete construction of the new schooner. The three masts were laid out thirty-five feet apart on the ground. One long eighty-foot spreader bar with three iron clamps was spaced to attach the masts. The large hoisting apparatus was attached to the center clamping device of the mast and the other end of the line was shackled to a locomotive engine. The commands were relayed from the tower that housed the winch to the engineer that powered the locomotive and the three crews to position the mast in the hull of the ship. As the locomotive engine slowly tugged the lines, the cable lines became taut through the tackle blocks and started to raise the masts. The signal was re-layed to hold fast as the engineer coasted the locomotive to stop.

The superintendent yelled to each foreman, "Check the lines and clamp them tight!"

Each foreman in turn checked the cable made of stranded, wire rope of two-inch diameter for frays and cuts as the cable wound through the huge block and tackle. There were eight sheaves in this block which Hjalmar had meticulously designed and fabricated in their shop for this job. It took six months to fabricate the beast, as it had been nicknamed. The test of trial and error was over, and now the true test of integrity of the beast was about to take place. Sling straps make a double choker which was attached to each end of the spreader bar. There were three crews within the hull of the ship to position the newly made masts. Ten men and a foreman made up each crew. The superintendent relayed signals to the locomotive engineer to chug forward and hoist the load. As the masts were hoisted in midair, lines hung suspended from the bottom of each mast. Each crew grabbed for the suspended lines to guide the masts into position. The crane pivoted into position and a cog wheel jammed against a misplaced awl that brought the crane to a dead, jerking halt. The heavy load swayed in midair as the cable snapped causing a calamitous moment. Three masts came crashing down upon the unsuspecting crews, crushing and killing fifteen men and injuring most of the other crew. Horrified, Hjalmar could barely pull the steam whistle that was attached to the tower to signal any mishap or emergency. It had been five years since the last tragedy when the uprights supporting the hull of a ship gave way crushing five unsuspecting souls to death. Now peering down from the tower, he was paralyzed to react quickly as screams of anguish echoed from the peril. Crews came running helter-skelter from every which way within the shipyard to aid in the rescue. The whole episode became so surreal for Hjalmar that he couldn't fathom the multiple deaths. Life is a precious gift and anything that threatens life can give us a new perspective on just how fleeting life can be.

Gustavus heard the alarm as he stood on the porch of his home which overlooked the bay. He rushed to the barn to saddle his horse. Galloping at full speed, his only thoughts were of his boys and brothers that worked at the shipyard. Upon arriving on the scene, it was complete pandemonium. Looking over towards the tower, he could see Hjalmar seated on the ground at the bottom of the tower holding his head in the palms of his hands.

Shock had seized him, and Gustavus sized up the situation, barking out commands to the remaining crews to, "Disconnect each mast and get the portable cranes in place!" He knew that the only way to rescue any survivors was to handle each mast separately. Wasting no time, he quickly resumed command, "Form three crews —- get the stretchers and Johnson bars; heave ho and get each mast off those bodies!"

The grimace on his face foretold the strain on Gus, as he was called by his friends, as he barked out more commands, "Head count!"

Each man that worked at the shipyard was assigned a number and was cautioned to yell out their number whenever a catastrophe occurred. Gus knew that Svante and Lucas numbers were 42 and 43 and listened intently as the roll call proceeded. As he heard the numbers echo out, a sigh of relief came over him when he heard number 42 and 43 resound. Now what about his brothers?

Each mast was heaved ho and dragged off by a team of horses. Gus climbed down into the open hull of the ship, and his eyes scoured each body as he searched for his brothers. Again, taking charge, he said, "Load the wounded carefully in the wagon and take them to the hospital—- get a doctor here – the rest of you remove the dead and cover their bodies!"

Walking towards a row of bodies, Gus recognized many of the dead men lying there. Then he stopped dead in his tracks for there was Gudmund, one of his brothers. He was still trying to hold some composure, for he knew someone had to be in charge, for the three foremen were instantly crushed to death. There was still much commotion as crews raced back and forth, trying to save any remaining soul.

Tears streamed down his face as Arvid and Einar approached him. With mixed emotions, he hugged his two other brothers. God willing, they were alive. Out of the chaos some order was established and all the bodies were removed. Seventeen able men were killed by the tragedy, for two more workers died on the way to the hospital. Gus walked over to Hjalmar and tried in vain to bolster him up with, "Come on, H, and pull yourself together!"

Hjalmar, or "H" as he was known among close friends, was a good friend, for the two of them had shipped together and gotten out of many close scrapes with death. "H" was hardbound, impenetrable, and often considered a visionary amid his coworkers. With clear vision, precise focus, and unyielding determination, Hjalmar founded the shipyard and built it into an amazing establishment. Now the fate of the shipyard was out of his hands because he knew all too well that this would be the end. Between loss of manpower, trust, and cost of the catastrophe, it was inevitable that the shipyard would close. Perhaps it was time for a new vision, a new dream, and as he gazed westward, he wondered if America was that place to fulfill a new dream?

Time is often needed to heal the wounds of life, but time is also of the essence for prayer and reflective thought to discern what steps are necessary to either overcome or rectify the tragedies in life. As time and days progressed, it was inconclusive how that awl was found wedged in the cog wheel of the crane. Industrial espionage was a common practice among the shipyards but not sabotage.

Ideologies and friendship intertwined strong bonds of a common thread and right now Gustavus realized change was in the wind and "H" needed his help. With the closure of the shipyard and economic decay becoming prevalent, Gustavus made plans to tell "H" what he had in mind. Now as he approached the steps to Hjalmar's home, he turned to look back across the shimmering sea and tears came to his eyes. Sweden was a beautiful land, the largest of the Scandinavian countries and the most populous, sandwiched between mountains and Norway to their left and Finland to their right. Northern Sweden takes you as close to the arctic circle as possible! The country of ice-hockey and downhill skiing comes with old names of tradition based on Vikings and Norse mythology. For Gustavus meant "staff of the gods" and Hjalmar, "fighter with a helmet," now his heart grew heavy with melancholy as he knocked on the door. He was warmly greeted and over a couple of vodkas, the plan was revealed.

Det Fyra Vindar, the four winds, a beautiful clipper ship owned and operated by Gustavus now wanted to sail his family along with anyone else that wants to go to America. The proposition aroused and even excited "H" as the plan was relayed to him about the adventure. A new way of life awaited them and their families if they had a passion to go, to start anew! It was the beginning of a new era for even the clipper ships were being replaced by steam ships. Smoke stacks billowing versus sails a blowing in the wind as they both agreed that the time was now to build a new life. So, it was settled, and preparations began in earnest.

The clock tower struck midnight as Axel and Stefan escorted their brothers Otto, Kurt and Wolfgang to a barge that awaited them on the Werra River. The rivers Werra and Fulda converge to form the Weser River in north-western Germany which meanders some 281 miles through lower Saxony, northward towards the North Sea where tall tales abound and fairy tales began. Night passage awaited them bound for Bremen where they would exit the barge because this would be the first checkpoint for stowaways, then a short overland trip to the busy seaport of Bremerhaven where the steamship, SS Freiheiten Suchen, Freedoms Quest was bound for America. Many emigrants left Germany during this period with high hopes and aspirations for a better way of life.

Otto adamantly objected, "No, Axel, I want to see Mama and Papa before we leave. I just can't go this way; it's been too long already since I've last seen them both!"

Axel threw up his arms in utter frustration and protested to Otto, "You run the risk of being arrested and thrown into prison! And Papa could be executed for aiding the clergy! Is that what you want?"

In utter grief and disbelief, Otto could not understand how in a country that he loved so much, how could such infamy exist. As in any long, culture struggle the innocent and helpless pay the terrible price, for many will die so that others may live. Feeling completely dejected, Otto knew down deep that Axel was right as they proceeded to the barge.

It was a bitter, cold day in mid-April as the barge made the transit along the Weser River. Kurt and Wolfgang could not stop shivering as their teeth chattered and they tried in vain to rub their hands to warm themselves. It took four days to journey to Bremen and hide in a warehouse until nightfall before they could carefully proceed to Bremer-haven. The city council of Bremen passed ordinances back in 1832 that required all companies transporting emigrants to file a list of all passengers with the city's emigration department. But through the years the accumulating silt in the river caused Bremerhaven to become the embarkation point for most emigrants leaving Germany. Axel had diligently gotten the papers for Kurt and Wolfgang but forged papers for Otto under an assumed name, hence the reasoning behind hiding out in the warehouse. All religious individuals were being checked, and until he was safely aboard and bound for America, every precaution had to be taken. Axel had also arranged for papers through the agent in Witzen-hausen for Stefan, who would accommodate his brothers to America. Axel, being one of the older brothers, would remain behind to look after Mama and Papa as well as the rest of the family. Anxiety and emotions surged as they approached the Freiheiten Suchen. She was a beauty with two smoke stacks and four masts, built during the era between sail and steam. This baby could cross the Atlantic in 14 days, whereas most sail ships took eight to ten weeks. Sailing vessels had to pack more supplies to make the duration so it was a no brainer when the steam ship came along.

Axel became a little downtrodden as he hugged his brothers goodbye but relieved that the ship would be leaving on time. Due to weather, loading supplies and boarding a maximum number of immigrants, most ships never left port on time. Most ships could be two to three weeks late and with the authorities checking for false IDs, Axel breathed a sigh of relief as lines were cast off. Altogether there were some 165 immigrants plus crew to make the crossing. Stefan stood along the rail with Kurt and Wolfgang and looked down upon the well-wishers waving, but Otto backed into the shadows of the darkness to hide his tears as he could not bear the goodbyes. He had become a man of great personal integrity, dignity, and sensitivity that he learned from the values of his family upbringing.

Axel blended in with the crowd as he stood on the dock with other families and well-wishers waving and singing the song of Germany, which would eventually with some changes to the verses become their anthem in years to come.

"GERMANY, GERMANY above all things,
Above everything in the world,
When, for protection and defense,

It always stands brotherly together.
German loyalty, German song
Shall retain in the world
Their old beautiful chime
And inspire us to noble deeds
During all our life.
Unity and justice and freedom
For the German fatherland!"

The ship pulled away from the dock, and Axel waved even harder as he yelled, "Auf widersehen, my brothers!"

Goodbyes and farewells are never easy. Axel turned to walk away for he couldn't bear to watch the ship depart.

Chapter 2
Sails to the Wind

Adjo and Farval are the Swedish terms for goodbye and farewell, but there were no dramatic send offs or goodbyes from their native land. On April 27, 1874, it was sails to the wind as the clipper ship, "Det Fyra Vindar," the four winds, set sail at high tide for this land known as America. Sunrise was peeking over the horizon and as always sunrise and sunsets were exhilarating to Gus as God's marvelous creation came alive each day on the sea. There is nothing to compare the brightness of the sun or the fairness of the moon shimmering across the sea accentuating each billowing wave. The tantalizing unknown excited Gus for what lie ahead as he watched his sons climb the rigging to unfurl the sails. A strong breeze came from the starboard side, still chilly from the winter winds as he rubbed his hands vigorously to warm them. It was an opportune time to pull up stakes and set sail for America, for nine years had passed since Robert E. Lee surrendered and reconstruction of the United States was well on its way. The transcontinental railroad was completed and that golden spike connected the Central Pacific and Union Pacific lines. Although, there were troubles brewing in America, just as in Europe, as Jesse James and his gang robbed their first passenger train in July of the previous year. It would be two more years before Alexander Graham Bell patented the telephone and the familiar sound of "Can you hear me now?" would echo from state to state. By now there were some thirty-seven states admitted to the union. The push to expand westward was ongoing by wagon, train, or ship, and the melting pot had an insatiable appetite for many more settlers.

Gus always felt awkward when he was landlocked but once on the sea was at peace and at home. Traveling to America reinvigorated Gus and intrigued him with suspense for what laid ahead for their future. What new persons, events, and trials awaited them in this new land and more importantly the suspense of rebuilding their lives for a better life? Life at sea all those years away from family left a burning hole in Gus's heart, and he wanted with all gusto to begin anew to rebuild a better future for his boys. With sails unfurled and a steady wind, the *Det Fyra Vindar* made good speed as she sailed pass Gotland Island in the Baltic Sea. She was well named for most ships had three masts but the *Det Fyra Vindar* had four masts and another advantage. The traditional square-rigged ship had five mainsails per mast but this one had six with two top royal sails to accommodate for faster knots at sea. Now her true trials of survival at sea would begin as the pirate frigate *Besposhchadnyy* came into view. The frigate *Besposhchadnyy*, Russian for "merciless," sailed with a cut-throat crew that plundered and left no survivors, just fear on the high seas.

The vicissitudes of life can cause the common good of most peoples and nations to falter at their best. Russia during the 1800s suffered from too many wars, excessive taxation, civil unrest, loss of liberty, poverty and dislocated peasantry. From loss of liberty arose complacency, apathy and piracy became a way of life for many. From the ashes of corruption, a group known as the Razin Marauders plundered along the Baltic Sea.

Hjalmar, scanning the horizon with his spyglass, was the first to notice the *Besposhchadnyy* and relayed word to Gus that trouble may be brewing. Both knew all too well from firsthand experience about piracy on the high seas. Gus came scurrying to the stern of the ship and asked H, "How do you know their pirates?"

H, still surveying the frigate heatedly, responded, "No flags are showing and there are guns mounted along the deck!"

Gus began yelling, "All hands on deck!"

Gus began commanding "Tighten all sails; secure all sheet lines and halyards! Let's out run these bastards!" a passionate Hjalmar exclaimed.

The *Besposhchadnyy* was about two kilometers off the port side. With the extra sails and God Speed, they would try to make the Danish Isle of Bornholm. Danish Navy ships docked at times at the port of Svaneke to combat any maritime calamity.

Gus smiled to himself as his sons glided through the air, swinging on lines to tighten the next sail. Then as he watched his boys grapple with the sails, life and this hostile encounter, he realized that his sons were no longer boys but had grown to be young men. He got a lump in his throat and a sense of pride just watching his sons.

Hjalmar's eyes scoured the horizon west for the Isle of Bornholm, but to no avail, for there was no land in sight. He quickly turned and focused his eyeglass east towards the *Besposhchadnyy*. She was gaining speed and bearing some five hundred meters off their port stern.

Hjalmar yelled to Gus, "Gus, fire two gun shorts to the west!" Hjalmar was hoping to alert the naval authorities at Svaneke of their peril but wasn't sure of their location from the island without looking at the navigation charts.

The steam frigate was steadily gaining on the *Det Fyra Vindar* as Hjalmar scurried below deck to check their position with the navigation charts. The last position plotted with the sextant was about hour ago, sliding the parallel rule along the chart and extending their course line located their ship close to the island, no more than five kilometers away. With all sails to the wind, they just had to make the trek and as fate would have it survive another ordeal. Not many get a second chance in life, and both Hjalmar and Gus wanted a better future for their families. It could not end like this for their fate would be sealed if the Russian frigate over powered them. They were no match for the gun power of their adversary as the frigate veered to the starboard side of the *Det Fyra Vindar* to bombard her with their cannons.

Gus shouted to "H," "We need sharpshooters aloft!"

The only way to survive this piracy threat and avert disaster was to kill as many pirates as possible. Hjalmar and his brother Milo were both sharpshooters in the service, and Gus could hit a bull's-eye at 100 meters. With their Lorenz model, long range rifles, each man climbed a mast to the crow's-nest and positioned themselves for the onslaught! Climbing the mast with rifles strapped over their shoulders in rolling, thunderous seas was treacherous. Lining up a culprit in their sights, expediency was paramount as the frigate came in sight off their starboard side. Shivering from the cold, fingers numb from the sea spray, Gus fired the first shot followed by a volley of gun shots from Milo and "H." Each of them hit their mark as they reloaded, positioned and fired again. A thunderous roar echoed from the canons on the *Besposhchadnyy* causing devastating damage to the side of the *Det Fyra Vindar*. A direct hit broadside put a sizeable hole just above the water line. Quickly reloading, Gus fired again and hit a powder keg which exploded causing much damage on the frigate. Hjalmar aiming for one of the pirates hit his mark and then turned to eye Milo before reloading. Milo, hanging over the crow's-nest from his fatal wound, was motionless as "H" yelled below for some assistance for Milo. Another barrage of cannon shots could be heard but in the distance and not from the *Besposhchadnyy*. Looking west, "H" could see two naval vessels racing towards their position to give aid. Once the pirates got wind of the Danish Navy, their vessel came about and skedaddled as fast as the frigate could go but it was no match for the faster naval vessels. Both naval vessels followed in hot pursuit and the lead vessel fired one round ahead of the *Besposhchadnyy*'s bow to give a warning shot to stop their engines. Pirates never cease and don't have the brains to give up as they tried in vain to out race both naval vessels. Once the naval proprieties were met and the *Besposhchadnyy* failed to stop; the KDM Frederik IV readied her guns and came upon the starboard side of the frigate while the KDM Norske II readied their guns on the frigate's port side and blasted away. Within three and a half minutes, the frigate sank out of sight without any survivors. A fitting end for the merciless!

The naval vessels then proceeded to the *Det Fyra Vindar* which was towed to the port of Svaneke for repairs. Milo was taken to the local hospital and for now holding on by a thread of life. His life was in the hands of God and the local doctors. A precarious beginning for the *Det Fyra Vindar* but with each challenge in life, choices need to be made and change was brewing in the wind.

As for the steam ship S.S. *Freiheiten Suchen*, it has been an uneventful, calm nine days at sea with high anxiety and new dreams for arrival in the destine port of New Orleans. Freedoms Quest was a lot more than just a name for a ship; it was also the hopes, dreams and destiny of 165 immigrants bound for this new land. As Otto walked around the promenade deck of the ship, he looked up at the gigantic smoke stacks and high mast with sails flapping in the wind. How did everything transpire to this crossing of the Atlantic, he was supposed to be coming home to see family and friends and be ordained in his hometown to begin a spiritual life as shepherd of his own flock? He slowly turned and watched his older brother Stefan giving some counsel to Kurt and Wolfgang. Coming home, Otto felt so self-assured and ready to be pastor but now was lost as he moved towards the ship's rail to brace himself to get on his knees and pray the Lord's Prayer for some comfort:

Vater unser im Himmel,
geheiligt werde dein Name;
dein Reich komme;
dein Wille geschehe,
wie im Himmel so auf Erden.
Unser tagliches Brot gib uns heute.
Und vergib uns unsere Schuld,
wie auch wir vergeben unsern Schuldigern;
und fuhre uns nicht in Versuchung,

sondern erlose uns von dem Bosen.

Denn dein ist das Reich und die Kraft

und die Herrlichkeit in Ewigkeit.

Amen.

Life's journey can certainly be an awakening spiritually, as Otto got up, planted his feet firmly on the deck of the rolling ship and felt reassured from above that all would be alright. He now moved with a self-confidence as he met the first family, Ernst and Emma Schmidt along with their sixteen children. Next, he met the Meyer family along with their eighteen children and the Richter family with their ten children. They wanted land to farm and the Homestead Act of 1862 promised 160 acres to able settlers if they had the will and backbone to develop their own land. Prior to the Homestead Act, tracts of land were originally given at 640 acre tracts and then reduced to 320 acre parcels. But due to the countries industrial and urbanized development and 180 million acres granted to railroads to expand west, homesteads would now only be 160-acre plots.

Without being cognizant of his own instincts, Otto was already cultivating his fatherly way of becoming a true shepherd. Smiling to reassure the families that all is well, Otto continued to move along and introduce himself and learn a little more about each family. There were some nineteen families in all with one common goal to start anew and make America home. What forces were at work to mold new generations of people from so many cultures into becoming an American and seeking this new way of life? Otto was re-energized from above and from each family that he met as he continued along the promenade deck talking to the Bergmann family who already had relatives living in New Orleans. Just a short hike and a stone throw away was a body of water known as "Lac des Allemands," which is French for "Lake of the Germans." This area, which to this day is known as the German Coast, was owned by a Scottish developer who was seeking workers by promoting his holdings in war-torn Germany. These hard-working Germans left a legacy of feeding the struggling settlement of New Orleans, helping it to survive and above all introducing that magnificent sound of the accordion into Cajun music. God surely loves His happy, good people and God loves a good polka and a terrific Cajun Jig! The Bergmann family, with eager anticipation, was looking forward to settle there. Then Otto met the Schusters and Krugers, who also had relatives living there and working in the local breweries which flourished since the 1850s. In fact, there were some thirty breweries, each with its own nuance of beers and cheers for every occasion as the sounds of "Prost, Trinken, Gutes Leben," that is, *cheers, drink, good life*, echoed throughout New Orleans. This happy occasion of meeting neighbors and getting acquainted was also an epoch journey of a greater understanding of who we are and ultimately where we come from. For a people of faith, which is not indigenous of any one nation, have a more ardent zeal and a determination to build again a better life and help their neighbors along the way.

As Otto moved along to meet more of the families, a thunderous explosion jolted the ship which startled the crew and panicked the immigrants. The chief engineer being badly burned from steam struggled to carry the only survivor from the engine room topside. The captain and first mate came running down the deck to give some assistance as the chief engineer, who was a courageous man tried in vain to proceed back to the engine room to check on the rest of the crew. Boiler explosions were a new peril at sea and during the transition from sail to steam propulsion there were few people that could contend with these dangers. The very first scotch marine, fire-tube, boiler was built in 1862 and the technology for safety devices wasn't adequately developed yet. When a boiler explodes the steam, which is under pressure, it expands so rapidly once it contacts atmosphere that anyone near the explosion would die immediately. Your lungs would collapse and you would be cooked like a boiled, Maine lobster.

The captain quickly fathomed the tragedy as he yelled out the commands to his crew to assist in securing the engine room, properly remove the dead and unfurl all sails. The remainder of the trip would have to continue under sail. *Freedoms Quest* was only five days from one of the busiest immigration ports in America, New Orleans. With four deaths from the tragedy, preparations were underway for the somber events of burial at sea. It would be a tumultuous end to the voyage of *Freedoms Quest* versus the tumultuous beginning for the *Det Fyra Vindar*, the four winds, for major repairs were underway and Hjalmar planned for his brother, Milo, to be buried in the port of Svaneke. It was a heart rending time for "H" with the death of his brother.

The challenges in life cause change and choices to make that we otherwise wouldn't have conceived without the twist and turns that occur in our lives. We are weathered like driftwood from the waves of challenges and are either seasoned or desist. For now, the joint venture for "H" and Milo to build a new shipyard in America had to be put aside.

The somber procession of a funeral allows time for reflection of "what ifs" in our lives. Eight pall bearers carrying a wooden coffin, each in cadence without a verse, only the hollow, silent footsteps reverberate in the air as they proceeded to Milo's resting place. A plot of land was donated by the Danish military base for a fallen brother who had served in the Swedish Navy. It was a small procession of family and friends from the four winds that walked behind the coffin. Gus, his two sons and fellow comrades, carried the coffin to its final resting place. Milo's wife had asked Hjalmar to give the reading at the grave site. He pondered along the way what the reading should be and as they lowered the coffin, Hjalmar open his bible and began to read from the first chapter of Ecclesiastes:

> Vanity of vanities, all things are vanity!
> What profit has man from all the labor
> which he toils at under the sun?
> One generation passes and another comes,
> but the world forever stays.
> The sun rises and the sun goes down;
> then it presses on to the place where it rises.
> Blowing now toward the south, then toward the north,
> the wind turns again and again, resuming its rounds.
> All rivers go to the sea,
> yet never does the sea become full.
> To the place where they go,
> the rivers keep on going.
> All speech is labored;
> there is nothing man can say.
> The eye is not satisfied with seeing
> nor is the ear filled with hearing.
> What has been, that will be;
> What has been done, that will be done.

Hjalmar paused for a moment and wiped his sweating brow and then his tearful eyes before continuing, "Here lays Milo Karlsson, who was a true brother, a loving husband and father, and a courageous comrade. We, as humble servants, commend the soul of Milo Karlsson to our Risen Lord and Savior, Jesus Christ. Amen!"

The next two days were busy days to drown out sorrows and ready the ship to set sail once again. Between the funeral ceremony and the repairs to the ship, an unexpected two weeks had passed and change was once again in the wind. *The Four Winds* prepared to sail to Malmo, Sweden where Linnea, Milo's wife, and her four children would disembark and take the train partway back to their homeland of Gavle. Most of the return trip would have to be by horse drawn carriage. With pen in hand, Linnea wrote a letter to her parents who had remained in Gavle and planned to stay with them until she could reestablish herself. It took a better part of a day to sail from Bornholm Isle to Malmo and then another day for Hjalmar to see them off at the train depot. Hjalmar hugged Linnea and the children and found it difficult to put into words what he wanted to say. He felt guilty for coercing Milo to bring his family to America and now as he waved to his nephews and nieces, a surge of remorse overcame him as the train departed. Shakespeare said it best in his plays when he wrote, "Parting is such sweet sorrow."

It was good to be back at sea, for nature was God's tranquilizer pill for whatever ailed the human spirit. Hjalmar stayed busy with the nautical charts and Gus enjoyed teaching his sons the skills of using the sextant. A course was plotted to head north around the tip of northern Denmark and then proceed west to the North Sea. Readings of the sun and stars were taken every four hours and their position was plotted on their navigation charts. Once in the North Sea, then the Four Winds took a southerly tack to the English Channel and around the southern end of England. From that position, a course would be plotted westerly along 50 degrees latitude towards America.

Gus enjoyed watching his sons as they adjusted the sextant and first Svante would take a reading and then plot the marking on the nautical chart and then hand the sextant over to Lucas. They collaborated on plotting their course but didn't always get matched readings.

Lucas asked his dad, "Why don't our readings always match?"

Gus adjusted the pipe in his mouth so he could reply, "Well, to master the sextant requires some skill." His dad continued, "The more you practice, you will learn to eliminate the small errors."

Frustrated, Lucas asked, "But shouldn't our readings be similar?"

The dad, chuckling at him, answered, "Eventually. I'll split the both of you on different watches; Svante you will take the eight to noon watches and Lucas, the noon to four watches. When we arrive into Boston, you both will be extremely proficient as seamen."

Watches at sea were rotated every four hours, so if one was assigned to the eight to twelve watch, one would stand both the eight to noon and eight to midnight watch. Sightings or measurements were taken on every watch of the angle between a celestial object such as the sun, moon or star and the horizon.

Gus carefully instructed both of his sons on the art of conquering the ironmongery as he always called it, "When you look through the telescope, manipulate the arm so the star or sun can be made to appear on the horizon." Gus stopped long enough to watch them make some adjustments then continued with the lessons. "The trick is to make the celestial body just brush the horizon, which you must learn to develop into a knack."

Lucas, adjusting the arm and then the micrometer knob to align the object on the horizon, recorded the time in seconds, minutes, and hours. Then he noted the name of the object and its observed altitude.

Gus interjected, "Remember every second of time counts, for an error of four seconds equates to an error of a nautical mile in position."

Svante quickly interrupted, "Don't you mean in kilometers, father?"

Gus enjoyed their quizzical perception as he replied, "Remember, sons, we are going to America and must learn to work comfortably with both English as well as metric system."

At that comment, both of his sons grimaced for accuracy and time were of the utmost importance.

As the voyage progressed, both sons learned well the lessons on how to overcome the errors and adjustments of index error, dip and refraction to plot their course accurately. Within nine more weeks at sea, it became second nature to use the nautical tables to figure refraction and make parallax corrections. A pride radiated within Gus as he watched his sons strive, learn, and develop into able young seamen.

Before land was ever sighted there was a shout from the crow's-nest of, "Ahoy, whaling ships port side!"

The "golden age" of American whaling was at its height before coming to an end as kerosene replaced whaling oil for lamps and the tall tales of Moby Dick written by Herman Melville became famous around the world.

Now all were spectators on the *Four Winds* watching the antics of the renowned sleigh rides as crews from the whaling ships harpooned humpback whales before their very eyes. Whaling in Nantucket and New Bedford had become a highly lucrative deep-sea industry and a strong seafaring tradition off the shores of New England.

The *Four Winds* veered on a southerly course as both Gus and Hjalmar checked the navigation charts for the location of Boston. Both Svante and Lucas were on deck to take some final sightings. Exhilaration was at a high peak from all as the yell echoed from above of,

"Land Ahoy!"

And their destination loomed into view. On the nautical charts, it was just a point but 42.3601 degrees north latitude and 71.0589 degrees west longitude was Boston, a city of some 250,000 people from many nations and from every walk of life. It is now two years beyond the great Boston fire of 1872. Better than one million immigrants have come through the port of Boston during this period. This would be a new beginning for the Bergstrom and Karlsson families as they immigrated to America.

Chapter 3
Ceremony of Ordination

The dawn of July 4th, 1874: it has now been twelve weeks since the *S.S. Freiheiten Suchen* docked by the French Quarter known as the Vieux Carre, Old Square, which bustled with life from all points of the compass. All passengers aboard disembarked and became acquainted with the immigration process to America. Now it is a festive occasion for all with parades, fireworks, and picnics to celebrate the ninety-eighth birthday of the United States. Ulysses S. Grant is president of the United States working to reconstruct a divided country from the civil war, and along with steam navigation on the mighty Mississippi River, New Orleans soon began to rival New York City as the leading port in America especially for exporting cotton.

New Orleans, nicknamed "The Crescent City," which comes from a sharp bend in the Mississippi River at the French Quarter, enchanted all with her colorful history that covered all spectrums of the rainbow from just about all cultures of life. Nouvelle-Orleans as the French called it, founded this city back in 1718 and the early descendants of French and Spanish settlers are called Creoles as Kurt and Wolfgang learned, exploring this marvelous city. It wasn't until the Louisiana Purchase in 1803 that the United States took it over and influenced more governmental changes and industrial opportunities. It was once said in the Daily Picayune that there was no peace in the Crescent City due to the role of violence in the politics of reconstruction.

This was a slice of life that neither Kurt nor Wolfgang had ever experienced but they were enjoying all its provocative ways and innuendos of the night life. The courtesans beckoned as each young male strolled by, and Kurt found it intoxicating as one young, lovely lady pointed to him to come and taste and see for yourself. Her revealing negligee left nothing to the imagination which enticed Kurt but only embarrassed Wolfgang.

Wolfgang urged his brother, "Let's go back!"

But Kurt replied, "Let's go in for just one drink." The courtesan's spell had him hook, line, and sinker.

A major gazette once wrote about New Orleans as an exciting and fabulous city of charm, beauty and sophistication with its many restaurants, theaters and music. But oh, watch out for the many snares that lurk about for there are many wretched souls of thief's, whores and scoundrels to discard a body in the bayou of serpents and alligators.

Meanwhile, Otto had an appointment with the Most Rev. Napoleon Joseph Perche, third Archbishop of New Orleans, who had finally received papers from the Vatican on Otto Zimmermann with high praise and recommendations for his ordination with blessings. Archbishop Perche took a liking to the amicable ways of Otto and his firm understanding of the faith and more importantly the faithful followers. The interview lasted a better part of the day with the Archbishop consenting to ordain Otto on August 23rd, 1874 at the Cathedral of Saint Louis. In the interim, Otto would be serving at the Cathedral and learn which diocese he would be sent to, once ordain.

His three brothers were working at the docks loading cargo and learning about the intricacies of New Orleans. Stefan studied law back home in Germany and registered at the New Orleans University which was founded in 1869 for more classes to complete his studies. With the help of the Catholic Church all four brothers began the naturalization process of becoming United States citizens. That evening the four brothers were celebrating together over a supper of jambalaya, andouille and some crawfish etouffee. The camaraderie couldn't be any better, the food was fantastic, and the conversation was light until Otto asked the question on how were his brothers occupying their free time?

An indignant Otto looked at Kurt and exclaimed, "You were where and seeing who?"

Not believing his ears on what an unabashed Kurt was saying, a frustrated Otto blurted out, "A courtesan is just another name for a whore!"

Otto tried to regain his composure and then stared at Stefan with a quizzical look. Stefan, in a gesture of throwing up his hands and giving a chuckle, explained to his brother, "Otto, I can't be watching over them every minute between work and studies at the university, can I? Besides, Kurt is twenty years old and must learn some discretion about the wilds of life for himself!"

Just then Kurt turned to Otto and asked him, "How many women have you experienced, brother?"

Otto gazed at his brother and then with a sigh of relief replied, "For me things were different, I experienced a calling from an early age and knew that I wanted to enter the priesthood. And I wasn't around much those past six years while being at the Vatican for my studies. But I can assure you it is a life of fulfillment, and I am happy and content to give service to the Lord!"

"Yes, brother, but are you any good for giving advice on the amorous side of life?" Kurt asked sarcastically.

"Oh, my brother," Otto started to say with a sheepish grin, "life is full of all kinds of temptation and in God's wisdom He gave us only Ten Commandments to obey which has been a downfall for many to even try to obey them!"

"Well, then," Kurt earnestly asked, "what do you do when the hormones say yes?"

Now even Stefan and Wolfgang were paying attention as to how Otto would reply to that question.

Folding his hands and leaning forward on the table, Otto slowly replied, "I passionately pray for the strength to persevere."

Still being a little obstinate, Kurt pursued by asking, "And what if that doesn't work?"

Taking time to respond Otto said, "Then I take a damn, long, cold bath!"

With that reply, they all joined in laughter and Kurt got up and affectionately hugged his brother for he had proven to be the better man.

There are very few solemn occasions in life where the true meaning of bliss erupts forth and makes life worthwhile. Graduation exercises, weddings, the birth of a child, prayers to our Creator and Lord, church celebrations and funerals to name a few accent life and truth to give some meaning and purpose to our lives. There is no solemn occasion that tugs at the very heart and soul of an individual as when an ordination takes place because of the solemn profession to God with one's heart, soul and being which makes it so sublime. Everyone should experience at least once in their lifetime a Sancta Missa – Rituale Romanum for the Rite for ordination of the priesthood.

Otto had mixed feelings for the day of his ordination. Yes, there is bliss of joy and happiness but also sadness that his parents could not be present. He had received letters from Axel that his dad had been released from prison and was doing as well as to be expected. But Momma was failing with each passing sunset. The night before his ordination he kept vigil in prayer as thoughts of his parents tugged at his heart while keeping the heavenly goal of service before him.

Most ordinations take place on a Sunday, when many of the faithful can attend and participate more fully at a cathedral where the bishop presides. Otto was to be the only candidate this time as the procession proceeded into the church. The traditional rubrics of the mass with the liturgy of the word read, the presentation of the candidate and homily given by Archbishop Perche preceded the examination of the candidate.

Otto then stood before Archbishop Perche who questioned him, "My son, before you proceed to the order of the presbyterate, declare before the people your intention to undertake the priesthood. Are you resolved, with the help of the Holy Spirit, to discharge without fail the office of priesthood caring for the Lord's flock?"

Otto responded, "I am."

The Archbishop continued, "Are you resolved to celebrate the mysteries of Christ faithfully and religiously as the Church has handed them down to us for the glory of God and the sanctification of Christ's people?"

The candidate responded, "I am."

As the Archbishop continued to question Otto's faith in God, our Lord, the Church and preaching of the Gospel, his brothers were transfixed in their pews with awe and love for their brother. A deepening of one's faith in this life is never easy but by the Grace of God when it happens, it is inspirational to others.

Then all stood as the bishop invited the faithful to pray. "My dear people let us pray that the all-powerful Father may pour out the gifts of heaven on this servant of his, whom he has chosen to be a priest."

The ordination ascended in steps from the candidate kneeling before the Archbishop and placed his joined hands between those of the Archbishops to promise his obedience. Then prostrated himself as the Archbishop alone stood and sang, "Hear us, Lord our God, and pour out upon this servant of yours the blessing of the Holy Spirit and the grace and power of the priesthood. In your sight, we offer this man for ordination: support him with your unfailing love. We ask this through Christ our Lord."

Once again Otto rose and knelt before all and the Archbishop and all priest wearing stoles lay their hands upon the candidate for the prayer of consecration. After the prayer of consecration, the Archbishop, wearing his miter, sat while the newly ordained stood. One of the assisting priests arranged a stole on the newly ordained Otto and vests him in a chasuble. Next the Archbishop received a linen gremial and anoints with chrism the palms of the new priest while reciting to the congregation,

> "The Father anointed our Lord Jesus Christ through the power of the Holy Spirit. May Jesus, preserve you to sanctify the Christian people and to offer sacrifice to God."

As the mass continued with Otto assisting with the Liturgy of the Eucharist, all three brothers looked on in pride and felt humbled to witness the transformation of their brother.

The next few weeks were indeed busy, hectic, and uplifting for Otto as he met with the Archbishop and delegates to arrange for his future schedule to serve in the church, the faithful and at the local parochial school. He was burning the midnight oil when a knock at the door interrupted his train of thought as he was preparing for his first homily.

"The door is open, come on in," responded Otto.

Just then Stefan walked in and asked his brother, "What gives, it's past one o'clock in the morning?"

Feeling a bit frazzled, Otto said, "Working on my first homily, and it's not coming out just right!"

Stefan just smiled and put his hand on Otto's shoulder to reassure him and bolster his brother, "Look Otto, I feel sometimes your too much of a perfectionist! Remember back on the ship how you mingled and talked to the people to calm their fears? You are good with the people and if you just say what's in your heart, then your sermon will be fine!"

At that comment, Otto smiled and felt reassured as he turned out his lamp and both retired for the night.

That following Sunday Father Otto read the Gospel and then stepped forward and gave his sermon on the floor of the church and not at the podium in the sacristy.

His three brothers occupied the first pew in church and as he stepped down from the sacristy, Stefan gave a beaming smile to his brother.

Father Otto, folding his hands and then doing the sign of the cross, began his sermon with the name of the Father, the name of the Son and the name of the Holy Spirit and giving an Amen.

"My brothers and sisters in Christ, God loves you so much that He sent His Only Son to show us the way and the truth to everlasting life and to die for you and to die for me. It is personal for Him and it should be personal for you! God has two dwelling places; one is in His heaven and the other is in a humble and thankful heart. For where two or three are gathered in His name, He is always there amongst us."

As Fr. Otto continued his sermon, all were spellbound and very attentive to his words, especially the Archbishop and Otto's brothers.

Life is a precious gift and God has ways of accentuating that gift for each of us. For Otto had to leave both country and home and he missed his parents and the rest of his sisters and brothers. But in that transition, he gained a much larger family and closeness to his other brothers that could-n't be adequately expressed into words.

As Otto was settling into his priestly duties, Stefan joined the local metropolitan police department. At the time, there were some 3,500 policemen to protect the active city of New Orleans. He barely began his indoctrination process when a skirmish broke out that became known as the battle of Liberty Place which took place on Canal Street. An insurrection by the Crescent City White League against the Reconstruction Louisiana state government oc-curred on September 14, 1874. There were some five thou-sand members of the White League, made up largely of Confederate veterans, which took over the statehouse, ar-mory and the downtown area for some three days. Between the chaos and the insurgents inflicting about a hundred ca-sualties, the governor of Louisiana wired for some Federal troops for support. There was pandemonium among the city officials who didn't know exactly what to do. But Otto spoke to the Archbishop and to the city officials that this is a time to remain calm and trust in God before many more lives were lost.

One official adamantly barked at Otto, "My God, son, Hell has already broken loose!"

With the Archbishop's permission, Otto wanted to try and reason with the insurgents and save as many lives as possible. Otto hastily walked from the Cathedral to the statehouse carrying a white flag while praying the whole way, hoping that there weren't too many atheists amongst the insurgents. As Otto walked up to the front steps of the statehouse waving the white flag, a single gunshot could be heard. Otto froze in his steps, laid down the white flag, raised his hands to heaven and in a bold, loud voice prayed:

"Heavenly Father, bring peace where there is chaos,

Love for one's brother where there is hatred,

Harmony where there is discord.

We ask this through Jesus Christ our Lord and Redeemer. Amen!"

With that prayer, the White League insurgents peacefully retreated from New Orleans before the federal troops arrived and Archbishop Perche believed that he had just witnessed Otto's first miracle.

In due time Fr. Otto came to know the people within his parish whether they were catholic or not and the people certainly got to know him. His reputation grew far and wide and this pleased the Archbishop. Each week he would venture out to the various communities surrounding New Orleans and visit the Germans, the French, British, African natives, Creoles, Cajuns and undauntedly greeted and welcomed all; for aren't we all God's creatures?

During Otto's tenure at the seminary in Rome, one of his favorite authors was Henry Wadsworth Longfellow and his writings inspired Otto. He remembered reading the Evangeline which was about the fate of the Acadians. The French way back in 1604 settled Acadia, modern-day Nova

Scotia, cultivated the land, maintained a good relationship with the native Micmac Indians and became an independent stock not entering any local conflicts. When conflicts arose between the French and English, the Acadians remained neutral and would not bear arms. Due to this independence, they were exiled from their lands and scattered far and wide. Many eventually wound up in Louisiana where they intermarried and became known as the Cajun community. Now as Fr. Otto got to know many of the Cajun communities, he fell in love with these warm and benevolent people whom some outsiders consider to be too aloof. Some of the words of Henry Wadsworth Longfellow flashed back to Otto as he recalled the passage of, "Every man has his secret sorrows which the world knows not; and often we call a man cold when he is only sad."

Otto could only empathize with the Cajuns, for he too had been displaced from his country, home, and family. Time can be the healer of all wounds, but, as Otto was learning only, if quality prayer occupies that time.

In time Otto learned to veiller, pronounced "vay-yay," with the Cajuns or to shoot the breeze as one would say and picked up the slang of the Cajun tongue. His brothers, too, acquired the discipline and when one is displaced and inundated with other tongues gains a natural adeptness for new things, one of them being an acquired taste for their, "barbue," or catfish and Cajun moonshine. Ouch, "Oo ye yi," it could pack a punch!

The Mississippi River, due to her length, legends, and lure, enticed both Kurt and Wolfgang to a life on the river as they applied for the apprenticeship program for a steamboat pilot's license. It wasn't that long ago that another youth by the name of Samuel Langhorne Clemens received his steamboat pilot's license and piloted his own boats for two years. During that tenure, he picked up the term "Mark Twain," a boatman's call for noting that the river was only two fathoms deep, the minimum depth for safe navigation. When Clemens returned to his favorite pastime of writing, he used the pseudonym of Mark Twain for many years and gained much fame. Now with Kurt and Wolfgang struggling with English and learning about the people, places and nuances of American life, it was fascinating to learn that the Mississippi River spans some 6210 km or 3,860 miles and borders some ten states. In comparison to their largest river back home the Rhine only stretched some 764 miles long.

It was Mark Twain that once said, "The secret of getting ahead is getting started."

And so, both Kurt and Wolfgang got jobs on different steamboats to gain a vast knowledge of the ever-changing river and the hundreds of ports of call along the way. It was a very precarious life on the river between the murders, muggings and explosions. In fact, during the 1800s there were better than 4,000 fatalities on the river due to boiler explosions. And some five hundred vessels were wrecked by this peril. Vessels were not inspected, and safety was not a high priority with these early boilers being made of riveted, weak iron plate. These waters were unregulated which spurred on gambling, and unprotected which hastened many murders and deaths. But the lure of the river did not stop many from coming because it was the best means of transportation next to the railway. But there was also nostalgia to go from east to west and from north to south for the charm, beauty and intrigue of many of the cities such as New Orleans, Memphis, and Saint Louis. Kurt had seen a lithograph by Currier and Ives, which immortalized the great race between two steamboats, the Natchez VII and the Robert E. Lee between New Orleans and St. Louis in June of 1870. Now as he boarded the St. Louis Prize and his brother got a job on the Memphis Belle, both had dreams of their own excursions and river tales to live. Kurt blew the boats whistle to warn all onboard and along the dock that the St. Louis Prize was ready to depart. He manned the helm as the paddlewheel slowly churned up the waters and a bit of exhilaration overtook Kurt until the captain yelled, "Wrong way, dum- meee!"

Kurt quickly turned the helm and brought about the boat 180 degrees bound for Memphis. The first mate relieved Kurt for the currents got treacherous heading north and warned him to watch for oncoming traffic, the banks of the river and the ever-changing currents. He then told him to listen for the soundings when maneuvering the bends of the river as well as tracking our way on the navigation charts.

The first Mate counseled and cautioned Kurt, "Charts are only good for a reference point for there is nothing better than your eyes and a sharp mind for navigating the river. Things happen too quickly to be day dreaming; always be alert!"

Sound advice for Kurt and with that he enjoyed his first day on the river. The steamboat's first stop to offload cargo would be Baton Rouge before pushing on to Bayou Sara and Natchez. It would be another two days before Wolfgang's first trek on the Memphis Belle.

The Mississippi River became the very heart and soul of North America influencing life, war skirmishes, trade, and settlement towards the west. The steamboat added a color of glamour with it gambling, music and dancehall girls to the major cargo handling along its entire length and transfer of goods to keel and flatboats on its many tributaries. These weren't jobs for the faint hearted but for the rough, tough, extremely coarse, and violent frontiersmen with the illusions of being king of the river. The night before Wolfgang's maiden trek on the *Memphis Belle*, Otto met Stefan and Wolfgang at the Golden Plantation Restaurant for some southern cuisine and brotherly camaraderie.

Greeting each brother with a brotherly hug, Otto laughingly asked, "Well, how's our illustrious policeman and pilot to be doing?"

Wolfgang spoke first being anxious about his new job, "Great, just great, I leave tomorrow!"

"How long will your trek be?" asked Otto.

Wolfgang quickly replied, "About a month."

Stefan quickly joining in the conversation, "How long is Kurt's excursion?"

"I believe he told me about two and a half months depending on how much cargo they had to pick up for the return trip," Wolfgang added.

Otto, sitting back in his chair and with a reflective glance towards Stefan, said, "Our younger brothers are growing up, aren't they?"

Stefan replied with a sheepish grin, "Brother they were all grown and ready for the world long before your return home from Rome!"

Shaking his head and replying in the affirmative to agree with his brother, "I'm afraid that I've missed allot since my six years in Rome."

"And how about you, how is life as a metropolitan policeman?" Otto interjected.

A disgruntled look came over Stefan's face as he replied, "Disturbing!" Then he continued, "Each day there are about eleven killings and I swear that the city could double the number of policeman and it would not make a bit of difference!"

Fr. Otto replied, "My God, that is disturbing."

"What's needed are more priests to teach these heathens that killing is wrong," Stefan added.

"And that doesn't include the arrest for other wrong do-ings!" Stefan went on, "Yesterday we made some twenty-four-arrest beginning with a Mr. Zachary Dupuis, the mortician."

Fr. Otto, being intrigued, asked, "Why?"

Stefan shaking his head replied, "It seems that our dear mortician was not burying the dead and for the past twenty years gave a new meaning to the verse, 'Rest in peace!'"

Both Otto and Wolfgang were all ears as Stefan continued, "I'm afraid all those dead bodies became feed for the alligators on Trahan's Alligator Farm."

With that bit of conversation, a disturbed Fr. Otto said grace, ordered some wine, and they ordered supper.

After supper Otto told his brothers that perhaps he could shed some light on the way of death in New Orleans.

Fr. Otto took out his pipe, packed it well with tobacco, and then lit it and enjoyed the aroma, taste, and soothing effect of the tobacco before returning to the subject of funerals.

"Like New Orleans, the city cemeteries hide secrets of voodoo, ghosts and strange apparitions." Fr. Otto continued, "The cities way of death may be one of the most distinctive parts of its culture. For more than two hundred years now, people have housed their dead in above ground small tombs. The city back when it was first founded was always wet as it is today. The original site of New Orleans had a water table just beneath the soil and the land that slopes back from the river towards Lake Pontchartrain is below sea level. So, the problem has always been where do you bury the dead? And as the saying goes, there are as many floods as there are days of the week. This city has always known death from storms, hurricanes, and plagues of malaria and such where hundreds, if not thousands died. Above ground tombs became common to house the dead, and there became more tombs and cemeteries than regular homes. And every time there was a flood, coffins that were buried would rise and go floating by with a corpse. And every so often a corpse would sit up and wave as it floated by."

At that comment both Stefan and Wolfgang were laughing and banging the top of the table.

Otto continued, "May God forgive me for that whopper, for I got carried away with the story and I should not digress! Graveyards were created outside the city overseen by the priests of St. Louis Parish. The cemetery remained a prime burial spot for many years until it was filled. It became known as the St. Peter's cemetery. From then on all burials are above ground and some say that many spirits come out each year to enjoy the Mardi-Gras."

Fr. Otto stopped long enough to relight his pipe before continuing, "Now as far as the legend goes, there was a Bubba Trahan back in the 1700s that created some alligator farms to take care of the excessive dead. Do you suppose that this present farm is part of that legacy?"

Stefan just shook his head and asked his brother where he got all this information as Otto replied, "From the church archives!"

The following morning an eager Wolfgang, being able, willing, and ready, climbed aboard the Memphis Belle to the wheelhouse as Captain Josiah Vickery issued orders to have the engine room bring steam to full pressure.

Once Captain Josiah eyed Wolfgang, he issued orders for the First Mate to bring their apprentice pilot up to speed on the navigation charts. Their first stop would be where the Red River and Mississippi meet to transfer cargo of dynamite to flatboats. Dynamite was a necessary item to clear log jams from dead trees. The native Indians called it, "Bah hatteno" and the early French knew the river by Riviere Rouge. It was a constant battle for this major tributary to keep the passage open so supplies of coffee, beans and sugar could be supplied to Shreveport and Bossier City. The Red River had its own tributaries, the major ones being the Atchafalaya and Ouachita Rivers. Wolfgang found it difficult to pronounce and spell these words for the daily ships log itinerary and the First Mate just laughed and said, "Don't worry about the spelling or pronunciation, none of us can properly say these Indian names."

The First Mate continued, "Just take everything in stride and relax for there are more than 54 major tributaries and places to learn. For now, just divide this mighty "Missy" into two segments and learn the upper and lower one day at a time. I've been sailing her for nine years now and still don't have all the words right yet."

Sound advice for now for the Mississippi basin stretches from the Rocky Mountains in the West to the Appalachians in the East. Tributaries include the second and third largest rivers in the United States, the Ohio and Missouri, as well as numerous smaller rivers. Between torrential storms and floods, the river has changed her course too many times to count and learning to navigate this river was indeed a challenge for both Kurt and Wolfgang.

The brothers enjoyed their new home, America, even though each missed their homeland and family. Their new endeavors were challenging, intriguing, and stimulating as they learned their new trades— for Kurt and Wolfgang what it meant to be a riverboat pilot, Stefan to master the daily difficulties as a metropolitan policeman, and Fr. Otto, a caring priest learning to serve God and his parishioners. But more importantly, each of them had to learn what intentions lay in the hearts of men for not all were good!

Chapter 4
The Kennebec River

An upheaval, such as when a tornado or earthquake erupts, can cause such pandemonium, but the subtler upheavals such as a death or immigration can also cause much commotion from within. Each person on the Det Fyra Vindar, the Four Winds, had to contend with their own mixed feelings of melancholy and elation as they left their homeland, friends and culture for a new beginning in this land called America.

Americans encouraged relatively free and open immigration during the 18th and 19th centuries, and rarely questioned that policy because we were glad to welcome the influx of new peoples from all cultures. The Supreme Court hadn't passed any immigration laws or enforced federal responsibility until 1875 and so for now Gus, Hjalmar and their families, it was a simple and painless registration at the circuit court of Boston. The form was simple with:

May or may not be a slight entrance fee
One's nationality, place of birth
Ships name and date of entry to the United
States
Age, height, eye and hair color
Profession
Place of last residence
Schooling / health
Name and address of relatives they are joining
in the U.S.
Amount of money they are carrying

Forms were done in duplicate so the individual received a copy of the form as well as the circuit court of registration. Once the immigrants made it to their destination then each immigrant had to check in with the closest legal authority of that state.

Uncertain just where their destination would take them, new supplies were purchased to restock the Det Fyra Vindar. Hjalmar knew of some distant relatives that went to a place called Maine back in the mid 1800s but no known address, and Gus had relatives that immigrated to Quebec, Canada. So once the ship was resupplied, it was sails to the wind once again heading due north. Clear blue skies, strong driving winds and a warm welcoming sun greeted them on their short trek north. Sailing close enough to observe the coastline, it was dead reckoning all the way. Hjalmar enjoyed the rocky coastline of Maine and referenced the English Pilot, a set of four volume books, filled with charts, sailing directions and tables that covered Europe, the Far East and North America. He was captivated by such a beautiful coastline and the tall scented pine trees as he checked the navigation charts. It was calm seas and smooth sailing along the coast as the *Four Winds* passed many hamlets, fishing villages and rivers not noted on the charts. Unaware that they were passing the Saco River, for it is the site of a legend known as the "Saco Curse," in which a Saco Indian chief declared that the river would drown three white people per year in retaliation for harm done to his tribe, the *Four Winds* sailed by unimpeded. This place called Maine has more than 5,000 rivers carved out by glaciers in the last Ice Age, multiple rocky, jagged peninsulas that jut out into the sea, dotted with fishing hamlets and towns that reminded Hjalmar of home. Beautiful, breathtaking, and beckoning, it reminded him a little of Fjallbacka, which was a bit north of Gothenburg on the west coast of Sweden. Nostalgia tugged at his heart, causing his eyes to blur from tears as Hjalmar wiped them dry. He felt comfortable and right at home; somewhat bedazzled by its beauty and alluring charm as Gus put his hand on Hjalmar's shoulder which startled him back to reality.

Gus quizzically asked, "Are we daydreaming, H?"

Smiling wryly, he replied, "I miss home!"

Gus, shaking his own head in the affirmative, replied, "Ja, gor vi inte alla?" which means, *yes, don't we all?*

The winds were growing stronger as the day progressed, and Lucas noticed that the foremast was swaying more than usual. Climbing below deck both Lucas and Hjalmar inspected the footings of each mast attached above the keel. Hjalmar began by inspecting the foremast where it was attached above the keel and pointed out to Lucas the stress marks in the planking caused by the swaying mast. Then he proceeded to inspect where the mast protruded through the upper deck. Hjalmar, shaking his head, turned and warned Lucas that the stress marks will just get worse and cause cracks in the timbers if that mast isn't secured better. Walking aft, they finished inspecting the main, mizzen and jigger mast. Hjalmar turned to Lucas and said,

"I'll head top side and check the shrouds and stays while you tell your dad the condition of the foremast."

Hjalmar inspected the standing rigging, which supports the mast fore and aft. Athwartships, or across the beam of the ship, masts are supported by multiple shrouds known as ratlines where rigging at times can come loose. It took longer to inspect them and so he asked for some assistance from Gus and Svante. After a grueling thorough inspection, it was evident that repairs needed to be made.

Gus yelled to Svante, "Get your brother and the charts for Maine!"

Laying out the charts on the deck, Gus, along with his sons, scrutinized the charts looking for a good port to lay anchor. Thumbing through the English Pilot, Gus noticed a reference to a lighthouse that should be within sight of their ship's bearings. The *Four Winds* veered north and, approaching Pond Island on their port side, the lighthouse became visible, which was constructed back in 1821 and lit for the first time in 1855. Continuing their course with Hjalmar scouring the coastline with his eyeglass and each island they passed yelled to the helmsman, "Steady your course pass the Sugarloaf Islands both South and North on your port side."

"Aye, aye, sir," came the reply, as the helmsman changed course.

Gus and his sons, while furling half of the sails to reduce ships speed, couldn't help but reflect on the beginning of their journey. When they left Gavle the full complement of crew consisted of some five families of twenty-four people in all. With the death of Milo and the debarkation of Linnea and her four children, that reduced the crew to eighteen. Everybody pitched in to carry their own weight and all chores were divided out between the crew. The women worked in the galley making meals and making the ship home and as comfortable as possible. The *Four Winds* was ship-shape considering the twelve weeks at sea. Gus watched as his wife, Elsa and Hjalmar's wife Freja carried waste to the fantail to throw overboard. There was Hjalmar's daughter, Olivia being helped by Rasmus' daughters, Felicia and Leah to retrieve some buckets of water to swab the deck. Rasmus Bjornberg, meaning "bear mountain," was a huge man at six foot, eight inches tall and weighed close to three hundred and ten pounds. He had now worked for Hjalmar for some fifteen years at the shipyard. A good-hearted man and an easy tempered person but God help anyone if he got rowdy. He brought his wife, Ines, and their two sons, Isak and Theo along with their two daughters Felicia and Leah. Finally, there was Wilhelm, Wilhelm Axelson, Gus' First Mate and right hand man. The two of them have worked together now for some twenty-five years. He had his wife Cornelia and their three sons Sebastian, Oscar and Hugo which were fine strapping, young men.

Just then Gus' attention was captivated by the yell from Hjalmar, "Ahoy, channel ahead," while pointing to the entrance of the Kennebec River. Gus raised his hand to shade his eyes from the sun while looking east. Studying the navigation charts, Hjalmar noticed the notations for Kennebec River and Atkins Bay as they approached the point of land known as Popham. The river's name is Algonquian for "long, quiet water" named by the Abnaki Indians. Now everyone was scurrying from below to witness some old fort made entirely out of granite positioned on the point of land. Fort Popham was built in 1862 on the banks of the Kennebec to protect their capital from Confederate invasion during the Civil War. While the fort was never completed, it stands as a monument of testimony of the will of the people to defend one's rights. A couple of centuries back there was a short-lived English colonial settlement in this present-day establishment founded in 1607 and known as the Popham Colony. It was also known as the Sagadahoc Colony located in the present-day town of Phippsburg, Maine. Back then this territory was part of Massachusetts and was funded by the Virginia Company of Plymouth. Due to harsh, unrelenting winters the colony didn't survive as their more successful rival, the Jamestown Colony that was funded by the Virginia Company of London survived and flourished.

Responsibilities were shared as the Four Winds was piloted by Wilhelm at the helm, Hjalmar watching the channel and taking depth soundings, Rasmus and Svante ready at the bow to drop anchor and Gus shouting commands to Rasmus' sons and Lucas to furl all sails. Between the sails being furled and the *Four Winds* proceeding against the rivers current, the ship slowed to a snail's pace. The command was given to drop anchor and the ship came to rest in the safe harbor of Bath, Maine. The town was named by the postmaster, Dummer Seagull, after Bath in Somerset, England and was incorporated as a city in the mid 1800's. Unbeknown to any new immigrants about the Maine sense of humor; they were oblivious to the local colloquialism about the postmaster of being dumber than what, "Dumber than lub-star shit or seagull shit?"

It was a peaceful evening as the *Four Winds* laid anchorage in the harbor and the skiffs were lowered and rowed to shore. The four families enjoyed the evening ashore and the hospitality of the town as they all did relish the local cuisine of lobster stew, clam cakes and homemade bakeries. For most foreigners, the English language is difficult to master but add a bit of Mainiac to it, and it becomes mission impossible! Gus and all the others had a crash course in Mainiac 101. First, there are no -*ing*'s at the end of any words, just "N", "Fish-n, fight-n and box-n." Next eliminate all "W's" and accent the "R's." Instead of saying *I will write you a letter*, you say, *I will rite you a letter*. And instead of going *rowing*, you are going *roe-n*. Finally accent all "A's" and "R's" and exchange "U" for double oo's. One is not *climbing the ladder to the roof*, but *climb-n the laddar to the ruff*. And one does not *oblige* another person but *abliges* him. Ar-men!

In due time, Gus and Hjalmar could converse with the locals and communicate that they needed a foundry to make some repairs to the ship. The locals happily obliged him by pointing the way to Bath Iron Foundry which was founded in 1826. More recently it was purchased by a General Thomas Worcester Hyde, a civil war hero who had plans for the foundry. Upon finding the place, Hjalmar and Gus introduced themselves to a Mr. Thomas Hyde himself. It was a cordial visit, and they explained their predicament and inquired about casting some support collars for the mast and fasteners for the rattlins. Mr. Hyde agreed that the job could be done but it would take a few days to get the supplies from Portland and to get the castings ready. Over the course of the next few days, a Mr. Thomas Worcester Hyde got to know both Hjalmar and Gus a little better and genuinely liked both men. Especially when he found out that both men had previously served in the Swedish Navy and were officers of distinguished rank. Then when he found out that Hjalmar owned his own shipyard and that Gus was proprietor of his own shipping company, it was break out the Jack Daniels and drinks for all! It was rumored about town that Mr. Hyde liked these men so much that he was quoted as saying, "he had met many people in his time but never with the combination of an entrepreneurial spirit, ingenuity and wisdom rolled into one like a good cigar. By far these two men are the sharpest tools in the box!"

Autumn was approaching with fall colors and Mr. Thomas Hyde figured that with their Indian summer weather, this might be the last chance to have a clam and lobster bake at Popham Beach. He told Gus and Hjalmar that there would be wagons to fetch all from the Four Winds and escort them to Popham Beach on Sunday. The next few days were busy as the foundry drew up plans and prepared the castings.

The sun was high in the sky blanketing warmth over the beach; the wind was a gentle easterly breeze giving a comfortable day of laughter, cheers and good times. The food was scrumptious, the camaraderie was at its best and new friendships were cemented. And then to top it off during the evening, the fiddles came out as they broke into song and for the first-time Hjalmar and the rest of their crew heard the song of Maine.

"Song of Maine"

There is a beautiful haven; where I always long to be,
The scented pines grow tall, the rugged land and rocky coastline are hugged by the sea.
Where the four seasons live and the air has a mystical mist,
Rising from the ebb & current flow, this tranquil land really exists.
Where the mountains are free and the air is so crisp,
The forests are plentiful and the hoot of an owl proves it does exist.
The eagle soars high and the seagull glides low,
Eyeing their daily catch from the sea and rivers below.
Where moose roam the land, fish fill the sea and birds soar to their own charm,
The people are decent, peaceful, and don't ever mean you any harm.
A top of the morning and a gentle goodnight; fair greetings to all are always spoken,
Where values are held dear and some words may seem a little broken.
The smiles are sincere and the cheers greet you from far and near,

From sunrise to sunset this place we call Maine, God Bless All without fear.

Hjalmar closed his eyes as they sang the song and listened attentively with his eyes tearful and his heart nostalgic for that moment he felt right at home. Thomas noticed and watched how moved Hjalmar became as well as his wife, Freja, but kept the observation to himself.

The following morning one awoke to a chill in the air from the North winds sweeping down from Canada which revealed that old man winter would soon be calling, and it wouldn't be long before the land would be blanketed with snow. Gus and Hjalmar were discussing their options and wanted to wrap up the repairs to the *Four Winds*. Hjalmar now had reservations about leaving this place called Maine for he felt right at home.

With the castings completed and the final repairs made to the Four Winds that left one last option for a Mr. Thomas Hyde to speak to both men before their departure. He invited both Gus and Hjalmar to his home and over cordials of cognac revealed his plans for acquisitions and expansions to develop one of the largest shipyards on the east coast. And with such an undertaking of this magnitude, he could use their expertise and entrepreneurship as partners. As with any overwhelming offer, it is a time for reflection and not impetuous acceptance. Both men shaking Mr. Hyde's hand and thanking him for such an offer reassured him that he would have an answer in the morning and returned to the ship to discuss their options. With their past misfortunes, it was indeed a pleasing damn good offer to start anew not just for themselves but also their families.

Discussions went late into the night with them breaking the news to their family and friends. Then between Gus and Hjalmar speaking with Wilhelm and Rasmus and getting their input because this decision will certainly affect them all. It was an evening of surprises and reawakening emotions, first with Hjalmar breaking the news to Gus that he would stay and accept Mr. Hyde's offer. And that Rasmus and his family would also want to stay and work at the foundry. There was certainly enough money in the coffers between the two of them from their previous careers and half of the cash belonged to "H." But if Gus still wanted to venture on to Quebec and needed their help, they would continue the journey to help them and then return to Bath, Maine. Then after digesting the news from "H," Elsa walked in and interrupted their conversation. Hjalmar went up on deck to allow some privacy for Gus and Elsa.

"What is it, dear?" Gus interjected.

Elsa in a strained voice replied, "I need to speak with you before Svante does!"

A befuddled Gus looked at Elsa completely oblivious to what was going on and said, "By all means, what is it?"

Elsa approached the subject directly and got right to the point for she knew down deep how Gus would react to such news, "Your eldest son Svante will also be staying, and in December there will be a wedding."

Gus had to sit down and regain his composure for he was totally lost as to what was happening.

Elsa, to reassure her husband that the world was not coming to an end, said with a little smile, "It's ok, dear; you're a man, and you sometimes miss the subtle things in life!"

Gus threw his hands up in the air and looked totally bewildered and didn't know what to say.

Elsa, smiling, said, "You never noticed the morning glow on Olivia's face in the morning?"

A befuddled Gus just stared around and asked, "How, what – when did all this take place?"

Elsa, giving her husband a hug, replied, "Right under your nose, dear!"

Gus still acting confused asked, "But how?"

"Pheromones, dear, pheromones!" Elsa answered.

Gus shaking his head exclaimed, "What?"

Elsa, chuckling to herself as she left the room, signaled for Svante to enter the room and talk to his father while exclaiming, "You can talk to your father now that I have softened the shock."

Elsa, as she left the premises, was muttering to herself, "Mother was right; men cannot survive without a women's touch!"

As with most men in life, they feel that all things are strategically planned; then life interrupts us and changes our course!

After speaking with Svante and learning of a December wedding along with the expectations of a child due the following spring, Gus needed to go on deck and breathe a sigh of relief. Hjalmar leaning over the rail looking out across the river asked Gus as he approached, "How is the illustrious grandfather doing?"

Gus froze in his steps and replied, "Hey, you're right, I am going to be a grandfather!"

Just then at that moment all the bewilderment seems to have melted away and nothing else mattered. In every life, there are many forks in the road and one must choose which one to take. And one way is not always better or easier than the other but it does change your life forever.

With curiosity getting the best of Gus, he asked Hjalmar, "How long have you known about Svante and Olivia?"

Smiling at Gus, "H" just replied, "Everyone on board knew!"

Hjalmar looked over to his friend and, putting his hand on Gus's shoulder, asked him, "How long have we known each other now?"

Gus just looking at "H" giving it some thought replied, "Well, we went to school together and shipped out together, and I'll be sixty this November, so for better then some fifty years now!"

"You were the best man at my wedding; where did all those years go?" Gus asked.

Hjalmar replied, "Life, experiencing life!"

Hjalmar continued by asking, "Why is it so important to go on to Quebec anyway?"

Gus was stroking his chin as if to contemplate the question himself and answered, "My dad's brother, Uncle Allexander Bergstrom lives in Quebec. And a long time ago, he told the family that if anyone ever decided to come to the new world, and before making any major decisions to look him up and talk things over. He is involved in both politics and business and you know what that means?"

Hjalmar quickly replied, "Yea, trouble!"

At that, Gus just laughed.

The following morning the two men met with Mr. Thomas Worcester Hyde and Hjalmar accepted his fine offer with a hand shake and a coffer of 150,000 kroner to cement the partnership. Then Gus added an extra 50,000 kroner, explaining that whether near or from afar he would like to maintain a partnership if he could give his son a permanent job with the foundry. The joint venture was christened and launched as the Bath Maritime Trust. It would take years of hard work, acquisitions and development to see their dreams to fruition.

The following morning The *Four Winds* set sail for their new destination Quebec, Canada. Before leaving, plans were made to return in December for the wedding. And with the advent of a new addition to the family, Gus laid out plans for purchasing a cottage for summer visits. The ship hoisted anchor and, as the sails were unfurled, slowly headed out the Kennebec River towards the sea. Passing Fort Popham there were half of their crew, Hjalmar and Freja along with Svante and Olivia waving from the fort. Both Gus and Elsa were topside waving back with Gus exclaiming, "Life is a beautiful gift!" Elsa stood beside her husband just smiling with eager anticipation to hold their first grandchild in her arms.

The journey to Quebec would take a couple of days to Halifax, Nova Scotia for a short layover and another couple of day's transit on the St. Lawrence River to their destination. Nova Scotia one of eastern Canada's Maritime Provinces juts out North of Maine like a cap on a head. At that time in history Halifax and all of Nova Scotia were very wealthy holding trading ties with both Boston and New York. But after the American Civil War their reputation was slightly damaged for giving refuge to confederate ships. It seems that there was a split in loyalty with some supporting the north and a few of the merchants supporting the sentiments of the south. Huge profits were made by some supporting both sides selling supplies, selling arms, and allowing haven in the port of Halifax for repairs. One such confederate ship became a legend in Halifax known as the CSS Tallahassee which made a spectacular raid for nineteen days destroying 26 vessels along the Atlantic coast before hightailing it back to Halifax. After making major repairs to the ship, the *Tallahassee* made a daring midnight escape from northern warships by heading out of the harbor and sailing north. In the north of Nova Scotia there is a seldom used eastern passageway between McNab's Island and the Dartmouth shore. The channel was very narrow and crooked with shallow tides. The captain of the Tallahassee hired a local pilot to escort them with safe passage to avoid capture. It proved to be an interesting conversation over super at the Captain's Table restaurant in the port of Halifax for the crew of the Four Winds and a history lesson about the American Civil War.

The next morning it was sails to the wind with Lucas relieving Wilhelm at the helm. Gus watched as Sebastian, Oscar and Hugo trimmed the sails for a smooth departure. With such a small crew, Gus felt relieved that it would be a short trek to Quebec.

Arriving in the city of Quebec by ship as one passes the Ile d' Orleans gives a spectacular view that is a delight to observe with the lower town on the river's edge and the walled upper city on the bluffs with the Citadel on the highest point of Cape Diamond or "Cap Diamant," if you prefer the French pronunciation. Nicknamed the "Gibraltar of America," the citadel was built between 1820 and 1850 and is the largest British fortress in North America. The city is in both the oldest and largest of Canada's ten provinces which has a distinctive culture that evolved from the

French and English heritages. Quebec's name also comes from an Algonquian Indian word meaning "where the river narrows." Samuel de Champlain established the first permanent colony back in 1608 and as the Four Winds docked at one of the many wharves along the Charles River where it meets the St. Lawrence River to form the harbor of Louise Basin, history seems to come alive before your very eyes. Indeed, Lucas was enchanted with the panoramic view and charm of this old city and asked, "Father, what will we do first?"

"Well," Gus started to say, "we need to register and find Uncle Allexander."

Gus, pointing towards the west, said, "Beyond the walls to the west, are the provincial parliament buildings and that is where we can do both!"

Gus had Wilhelm and Lucas walk up to the street and rent a couple of carriages to take them to the provincial parliament buildings. Gus was rereading the last letter that he had received from Uncle Allexander which was better than a year ago, he was Minister of natural resources and was always looking for good people to serve.

Arriving at the steps of the provincial parliament building, Gus paid the drivers and proceeded to the west wing for court registers. Once registration for immigration was completed, the group proceeded to the east wing and asked for a Mr. Allexander Bergstrom. A distinguished, white-haired, elderly gentleman in his eighties briskly walked up, smiled and asked, "What's the matter, Gustavus, you don't recognize your Uncle Al?"

With rounds of introductions and some hugs that broke the strain of the initial awkwardness that years of absence bring, Allexander escorted the group to his office.

He began by saying, "I am glad and proud to have you all stay at our house and that includes you Wilhelm and your family. Clara, my wife, will enjoy the company of family and friends from the old country."

Then he eyed the boys and asked each of them what they would like to do? He quickly pointed out, "There are many options with fine courses at the university or apprenticeship programs for our many developing business ventures."

Then Allexander, turning to Wilhelm, asked, "I presume that you have enjoyed working for Gustavus all these years?"

"Absolutely!" was his response as he continued. "He is both a good boss and a true friend!"

"Good, good," was Allexander's response. "Then you wouldn't mind continuing to work for him as I think there are plenty of good opportunities for the both of you. After some lunch, I'll arrange for some carriages to take you back to the ship and get your things and then take you to our home. Clara will be so happy to see you."

Gus interrupted to explain that whatever the next steps are to take place, he would need a leave of absence in December to go to a wedding. He further explained about his son, Svante staying in Bath and along with his good friend

Hjalmar formed the Bath Maritime Trust. Allexander was indeed interested as he exclaimed, "Let me break the news to Clara and if she agrees, then we both should like to join you for the wedding."

Allexander continued, "And this Trust venture could be a good business proposition for both America and Canada!"

"As you move your belongings to our home, let me make some inquiries and arrange some interviews for the both of you over the next couple of weeks!" Allexander said as he clasped his hands and thanked God for their safe arrival. He was elated to be with family again and as a politician always seized the moment of a good opportunity.

Inspired by such fortuitous prospects, he outlined a list of people for Gustavus to meet beginning with Wilfrid Laurier who was a native of Quebec and studied law at McGill University. After three years in the Quebec legislature, he was just recently elected to the Canadian House of Commons. He was a staunch supporter of liberal immigration and wanted to build up Canada. A man of clear vision who demanded regulated transportation of both ship and rail and who would someday aspire to become Prime Minister of Canada. Then he added the names of the "Three Musketeers of Canada" for entrepreneurial development who were Alexander Tilloch Galt, Francis Hincks and William Cornelius van Horne who would someday become president of the Canadian Pacific Railway and CP Ships. It was a gamble that Allexander was willing to take for in looking for good people to hire, one looks for four qualities, integrity, energy, wisdom and vision. And if they don't have the first one then the rest is wasted. Allexander was confident that Gus had what it takes and that the other men would clearly see his attributes as well. There was one more name to add to the list but this individual was difficult to track down and hog tie sort to speak! There is this town located in Alberta, Canada just south of the North Saskatchewan River across from the City of Edmonton known as Strathcona. This town's recorded history actually begins now in the 1870s. The first residents were an offshoot of hangers-on, roll up your sleeves and dig in type of contractors and trail blazers who resided near the old Fort Edmonton north of the river. A mixture of pioneers, fur traders and farmers along with land speculators poured into this area like an overflowing river. Looking to expand Canada west and develop the town, Strathcona needed dependable transportation for a life-blood of supplies, goods and people. Now enters a Mr. Donald Alexander Smith into the picture who is a builder and financier of the Canadian Pacific Railway. In due time, he became known as "the grand old man of Canada" for he wants to push the railway development to the west coast right pass the door steps of this town, Strathcona. Now if Allexander could get the energy of Mr. Donald Smith and Gus together, the dynamic duo would help immigration, the railroad and the future of Strathcona. Uncle Al was always in his glory when concocting his deals. And above all if he could get the backing of these entrepreneurs behind Gus, then he was confident he could get the prime minister to appoint Gustavus as minister of transportation.

Over the next few busy months, the families of Gus and Wilhelm got settled into their own homes in Quebec City, Lucas and Sebastian registered for fall classes at the university and Oscar and Hugo went to work as apprentices at the shipyard. And a pleased Uncle Al, through the invaluable aid of his colleagues, especially his close friend Wilfrid Laurier, obtained an appointment for his nephew. The reigning Prime Minister, Alexander Mackenzie, was indeed impressed with the vigilance and adeptness of Gustavus and the entourage of his backers. For Gustavus made it a point where he was new to Canada to take the initiative and visit each man personally and press the flesh to introduce himself and win their approval. Gus understood the cliché all too well, do today what you can; for tomorrow is not a given! Upon his appointment as Minister of Transportation, he unhesitatingly made Wilhelm his deputy chief. Now the hard work would begin for uncompromising, phenomenal and enterprising ventures to build Canada to fulfill her visions and dreams.

The Hudson Bay being frozen over sent strong cold winds racing across Quebec Providence and temperatures plummeted in Quebec City showing a minus five and dropping. It was raw and bone chilling cold as plans were made to attend the wedding of a Mr. and Mrs. Svante and Olivia Bergstrom. Even though it was damn cold— how cold you may ask; colder than the hair on a polar bear's ass, that's how cold— it did not dampen spirits to attend the wedding. Arrangements were made to go by train from Quebec City to Portland, Maine and then a short trip by rail to Brunswick. Mr. Thomas Hyde planned for horse drawn carriages to pick them up at the Brunswick Depot.

During the scenic train trip at one point Gus asked Lucas, "How are your classes going in law?"

As a first-year law student he replied, "They are too tedious and pedantic!"

This caused a surprised reaction from Gus as he said, "Whoa, wait a minute and hold on son!"

Gus continued, "Law 101 is to teach you the basics and rudiments of the law."

Lucas replied, "Right."

Gus leaning over from his seat started by asking, "What is the purpose of law?"

Lucas responded again, "The purpose of law is to protect society."

Gus quickly responded, "And what else?"

Not answering quick enough, Gus replied, "To protect the individual's rights!"

Gus continued, "There is a fine line between society's rights and the individual's rights. And we have too many crappy lawyers that don't understand that or take advantage of it and too many legislators that pass terrible laws that infringe on both! When the laws don't work, they're either too lenient, or too stringent or worst yet did not cover all the bases!"

Gus sat back and took a sigh of relief before saying, "My best advice to you, son, is to learn the rudiments of law like the back of your hand."

Gus smiled and then said, "Learn to love the law because without it, we have corruption and chaos and no way to resolve our differences."

With that, they both enjoyed the rest of the trip.

The day of the wedding was beautiful, sentimental and memorable as Hjalmar walked his daughter down the aisle. That precious moment when the beautiful bride is first seen your heart soars with a joy and happiness that is unequalled in life except during the birth of your child. The ceremony proceeded and Svante and Olivia said their, "I do's."

The reception followed and everyone, including eighty-three-year-old Allexander and his charming wife Clara, got up and danced with joy. Indeed, it was a joyous time to celebrate for all.

The next two days went by quickly with the men congregating together to discuss what else but business and the women discussing womanly advice to each other. Brothers had a slight moment to exchange friendly barbs and brotherly affection. Mr. Thomas Hyde took the opportune time to invite a Mr. John Poor, a business tycoon from Portland to meet Gus and discuss future propositions. To establish healthy trade relations between countries and with the Bath Foundry Trust, there had to be better rail service to Bath. John Poor was the individual that developed rail service to Brunswick and had enough business clout to get things rolling for Bath. This was also a quiet, tender moment for Elsa, Clara and Olivia to talk about the finer, more delicate things in life such as relationships.

Elsa started out by saying, "Olivia, dear, love is beautiful and sublime, but reality has a way to, oh how do I express it, breaking the bough and bringing us back down to earth."

Olivia, still glowing from the wedding, said, "Why mother Elsa what do you mean?"

Slowly, Elsa started by saying, "Let me list the attributes of men, first a man's tongue can be as sharp as a cutting knife and cut through the flesh like a saw through wood.

Olivia, being a little flustered, turned and looked towards Clara as she said, "And she is putting it rather mildly!"

"Now, let me see," Elsa continued. "Men can be gentle but clumsy as a bear and as stubborn as a mule."

Elsa turning to Clara and asked her, "Is that how you would put it?"

Clara quickly replied, "I would have used as stubborn as a jackass!"

Elsa continued, "Words are not their forte but in their work, they can be a poet laureate. They can be quick tempered, drink too much, express opinions too much, have wanderlust and travel too much and those are their good traits! I think that sums it up rather well; what do you think, Clara?"

"You just summed up my husband to a tee!" replied Clara.

"Now, they are strong and dependable and can be as solid as the rock of Gibraltar; it's just that you need some dynamite to loosen them up every so often," Elsa said with some contempt.

Continuing, Elsa finally said, "Marriage is a delicate balance to allow the men to think that they are in charge and remember that men always forget and women always learn to forgive!"

Then Clara added a few more cents worth of advice, "It says in the Bible that men were created in God's image so God is a man! If God was a woman, things would have been much different! Just remember the female is born with sensibility and for a male it takes a lifetime to learn that!"

Olivia, being a little sheepish, now asked, "Can a man ever learn to forgive?"

Clara quickly answered, "Those that do, usually become a priest!"

At that witticism, they all enjoyed a good laugh.

Chapter 5
Last of the Indian Raids

The United States is a pioneering nation, land of the free and home of the brave to build liberty for all through three great frontiers. The first was the eastern seaboard in establishing the thirteen colonies, the second from the Appalachians to the mighty Mississippi and the third is the Great West, stretching from the mighty Mississippi to the Pacific coast. We are all immigrants or descendants thereof from every other nation around the world. Only the Indians can properly call themselves Native Americans, although they arrived from Asia many centuries ago. The burdens, sacrifices, and struggles to build a better way of life under the stars and stripes and a future for all lies in this last great, melting pot of America.

Four years have now passed and throughout the next decade the country sees the last of the Indian raids. By now Otto is elevated to a Monsignor with his own parish and is enjoying his flock. Kurt and Wolfgang are both full time seasoned river pilots learning more about life and the mighty Mississippi River. Stefan has completed his law courses and has received his degree while waiting to take the bar exam for the state of Louisiana. In the interim, he started his new job as a United States Marshal the oldest federal law enforcement agency in the land created by the first Congress in the Judiciary Act of 1789 under President George Washington. It was the Marshals that were given extensive authority to support the federal court system and execute subpoenas and warrants to apprehend desperadoes throughout the west. There were several gangs that brought chaos, fear, and corruption throughout the west by robbing banks, trains, and stagecoaches, wreaking havoc and disrupting life. One such gang, known as the Dauterman Gang, pulled many robberies from Texas, Louisiana and up through Kansas. A warrant for the arrest of Bart Dauterman and any members of his gang was issued by the federal court system and was assigned to Marshal Steve Zimmer. By now Stefan Zimmermann learned if he was ever going to Americanize himself, then he should shorten his name for a more comfortable pronunciation. He was to meet up with other U.S. Marshals in Memphis and travel under incognito to their destination. The Dauterman Gang was as ruthless and as bad as they come for their stickups left no witnesses. "Shoot them dead," echoed throughout the west from all parties concerned including and right up to the office of the president. The gang's shenanigans enraged the public with such an outcry that it was even being written about in European newspapers. Steve was always a good shot with his six guns, but he had learned in deadly encounters to rely on the old Henry Repeater. He made the transit on his brother's riverboat and enjoyed their short time together for it gave them time to chat.

Wolfgang asked Stefan, "Why did you ever become a U.S. Marshal?"

Stefan, scratching his head, replied to his brother, "Do you want the short version or the long?"

Wolfgang quickly replied, "We have all evening, neither of us is going anywhere else!"

"Well, you remember what happened back home in Germany with the Kulturkampf struggle?" Stefan started to say, "There were no laws to protect us and no judicial system to help us!"

"Yes," Wolfgang replied, "it was terrible!"

"That's why, I became a U.S. Marshal, here we have a judicial system to make a difference, and I definitely want to make a difference!"

In life's journey, we have choices to make before life makes choices for us and we must always remember that life is a gift from above and always try to walk humbly with our God to do what is right!

Steve and Wolfgang enjoyed their brief encounter and before Steve disembarked, he said, "Give my best to Kurt when you see him!" and gave a short wave as he disembarked from the boat.

It was a short trek to the Guzzling Gutsy Saloon where Steve would hook up with two other marshals who would be carrying Henry Repeaters as their ID. There were many saloons in Memphis, in fact there were more saloons throughout the west than anything else. One daily gazette had reported that there were 101 saloons to every 1 church. Mark Twain said it best, "Sometimes too much drink is barely enough."

Steve was told in no uncertain terms do not carry a badge and keep his appearance low key, for there were too many cutthroats and thieves in Memphis. If word ever got out that they were U.S. Marshals, all hell would break loose and the marshals would have to arrest them all. Once identified it was a quick meeting. A tall, lean hombre walked up to Steve and recognizing the Henry Repeater said, "It's a good day to be a Marshal?"

Steve replied, "Yes, it is."

While extending his hand to shake Steve's, he introduced himself, "My name is Earp, Wyatt Earp, and these are my deputies, Kent Vickery and John Bodie."

This introduction was long before his reputation became renowned at the notorious shootout near the OK Corral in Tombstone, Arizona with his brothers as deputies. Marshals back then could hire and fire their own deputies. But Steve scrutinized this individual unbeknownst of who he was or where he was from. As they traveled by train to Little Rock,

Wyatt revealed the plan to Steve that two more deputies would join them there before proceeding to Pine Bluff, Arkansas. This was the last known reputable information on the Dauterman's gang hideout. They were becoming infamous like the Dalton Gang and killed two Texas Rangers from a previous job in San Antonio, Texas. Strategically, Pine Bluff was an excellent location for a hideout with Texas and Louisiana to the south, Mississippi and Tennessee to the east, Missouri and Kansas to the north and Oklahoma to the west to hightail it in any direction.

Rutherford B. Hayes is now the presiding president of the United States with two thorns in his side and a withering reputation due to the major loss at Little Bighorn of 264 soldiers and a Col. George A. Custer and the depravity throughout the west caused by desperados under his term. He wanted one thing for his country, peace and then move on to a second term. That being defined, he issued an ultimatum to the U.S. Marshals, "to bring those desperados in dead or alive but, above all, get the job done!" History will show, he never made a second term.

Arrival in Little Rock was low key and clandestine, just quick enough to make introductions and pick up a set of fresh horses for a short ride south to Pine Bluff.

"Steve, meet Bass Reeves and William S. Tough, who will accommodate us to apprehend this gang," Wyatt said to Steve. As he looked at Bass, he said, "What about the Texas Rangers?"

Steve, being confounded, exclaimed, "What Texas Rangers?"

Bass Reeves, born a slave, moved west into the Indian Territory and became a Deputy US Marshal, working for the famous "Hanging Judge" Isaac Parker. Wyatt liked this guy because he was tough, mean and on one occasion he single-handedly arrested and brought to trial 19 horse thieves. He always got his man! And then William Tough headed west at the ripe old age of 17 and became a trapper, Pony Express rider and wagon master. During the Civil War, he served as a commanding officer and has now been a US Marshal for five years in Kansas. These guys were dependable and could shoot straight without blinking!

Wyatt continued to explain to Steve, "Texas Rangers are our Aces in the hole, and nobody gets away! We got two days to get there and a forty-mile ride, let's move."

The plan was simple without any illusions; the seven Texas Rangers would approach Pine Bluff at sunrise from the south end of town with the eighth ranger already in town keeping an eye on the gangs' whereabouts. The U.S. Marshals would approach from the north end and once contact was made start shooting.

Steve objected, "We will give them a chance to surrender, won't we?"

An emphatic, "NO," was Wyatt's only reply.

On the morning of June 25, 1878, two years to the day of the anniversary of Custer's Last Stand, the Dauterman

Gang stepped into the street from the Lucky Spur Saloon and were shot down by fourteen Henry Repeaters. The order that came down from the President of the United States was carried out expeditiously.

The nine dead bodies were loaded into a wagon and buried in unmarked graves as there was to be no fanfare or publicity, just an end to the gang!

Wyatt thanked Steve and gave him a writ for his pay as Steve boarded the Arkansas Valley River Boat and headed back to New Orleans feeling a little dejected. Steve believed in law and order and in the judicial system of trial by jury and he didn't become a US Marshal for this travesty of injustice and to swallow Wyatt's philosophy of, "It's either them or us!"

Otto enjoyed his parish, the congregation and the youth with all their adolescence concerns. There were two parochial schools within his parish district that he was responsible for the spiritual guidance and religious upbringing. Daily he would attend the two schools and circulate through the various classes to address any needs. Today he happened to be visiting the junior high classes and was in Sister Agatha's class as they were to stand for the pledge allegiance to the flag. He noticed that a couple of the students didn't stand during the pledge, but Fr. Otto remained motionless in the back until they were finished. Then he observed Sister Agatha's actions as she approached the two students to find out why they didn't participate. One of the students was American Indian and the other came from a family that believed that the south would rise again and suppress the blue belly swine. Sister Agatha, being very upset but unsure how to handle the situation, turned to Fr. Otto and was hoping for some spiritual guidance. Fr. Otto approached the sister and both students smiling and told both youngsters to take their seats. Then he turned towards Sister Agatha and asked her if she would mind if he spoke to the class. Sister Agatha sighed relief as the Father spoke to the class.

"Good morning, class," Fr. Otto began. He then continued, "We start each day by giving thanks to God in prayer and then we show our patriotism by giving our allegiance to the flag. It is important that we reflect and understand why we do that! I think it would be good for each student to shed light on why we observe that practice each day."

Then, turning to Sister Agatha, he said, "What do you think of a one page synopsis on those topics by each student Sister?"

Being pleased on the solution, the sister agreed with Fr. Otto and assigned the one page report to be due on Friday. After class Sister Agatha was talking to Fr. Otto about her family that both her dad and brother served in the Civil War and neither one came back from the war. That it was an extremely difficult time for her and her mother to cope with life.

Fr. Otto understood and said, "To paraphrase an old cliché, the pen is mightier than discipline. It will give them time to reflect and think out their actions." At that, Fr. Otto concluded his rounds and told sister that he would like to be back on Friday and sit in as each student read their report.

It was a beautiful, sunny morning as Friday rolled around and sure enough Fr. Otto was sitting in the back of class as Sister Agatha had the students one by one come up and give their reports. One report touched everyone in the classroom for it was done in the form of a poem. As Miss Bailey got up to read her poem, all ears listened attentively:

"We are born by the Grace of God with a life,
a soul, and a will, in the likeness of His Image
with courage for our hearts to fill.

From sea to sea and from shore to shore
we have fought through many wars, to defend, uphold and protect we try to strive by
our laws.

Too many have died and shed their blood
for God, home and liberty, strength and right is
our might and choices are made by our ability.

To strive and correct wrongs for the path
in life is never easy, through too many battles
of guts and blood to make us feel queasy.

We have been tested and tried too many
times to count, many lives have been sacri-
ficed as the body count still mounts.

The flag does not discriminate, but people do err to judge, too many feelings are hurt and too many people hold a grudge.

And so, to God we give prayer and thanksgiving for our Red, White and Blue, stand with Pride and show respect for our Stars and Stripes and all that is true.

Throughout the following weeks all students on their own volition stood and recited the Pledge of Allegiance.

The expansion west throughout this period was never ending and as families migrated further west, land became available once again in Missouri and other states. Even though the great migration west occurred between 1803 to 1860 due to the Louisiana Purchase and the Lewis and Clark expedition to uncover new territories, the year 1879 still saw many people heading west by wagon train and steamboat. That year a new steamboat, *the Montana,* was constructed to operate in the upper Missouri. It was the largest boat ever to traverse both the Mississippi and Missouri Rivers, and who was commissioned to pilot the new steamboat then none other, Kurt Zimmermann. Shortly after he started on the Missouri River, Kurt had a crash course on navigating, and he got a belly full!

From sunrise to sunset all he would hear is the gully waging Missouri slang of, "Just bee-kuse the Mississip is the biggest river in the con-tree, yu ain't the best boatmen, Bah! That's creek navigatin', yessiree-bub!"

Kurt to his demise learned that he got this job because no one else wanted it. Frankly, arguing about which river is the longest or largest is as futile and dumb as men arguing over which one has the biggest! "Dum-mees!"

In May of 1879 on board the *Montana*, he brought many immigrants to St. Louis and one such family was the Richter's who had crossed the Atlantic on the SS Freiheiten Suchen with the Zimmermann clan. Hopefully they were moving on to greener pastures. More families and supplies were loaded on board for their next port of call, Independence. Named after the "Declaration of Independence," this town quickly became an important frontier town because it was the farthest point westward on the Missouri River where steamboats could travel. Independence, Missouri is known as the Queen City of the Trails, because this is where all trails begin to head west on the Oregon, Santa Fe, California and Mormon Trail to just name a few. The steamboat powered along the Missouri to their last port of call known as Fort Benton, Montana where the largest delivery of some 600 tons was made.

The year of 1879 also saw many Indian skirmishes, deaths and battles before all Indian tribes were forced onto reservations. To name a few there were the White River War, the Ft. Robinson Massacre, the Sheepeater War, Meeker Massacre, Battle of Milk Creek, Alma Massacre,

Ute War followed by the battle of Big Dry Wash. Years prior to these battles there was an old Indian chief Known as Chiksika of the Shawnee Nation who once said, "When a white army battles Indians and wins, it is called a great victory, but if they lose it is called a massacre."

The irony in settling the west is that we destroyed one culture to make room for others and we could have learned so much from the various Indian tribes. Who can fathom except God, the very depth of their spirituality that had been destroyed? In the following decade from 1891 to 1898 were the last Indian uprisings with the Battle of Leech Lake considered the last Indian War in America?

The Montana departed Fort Benton and steamed along the Missouri not knowing what lurked around the rivers' bend. A small band of Indians from the Piegan, Siksika, and Kainai Tribes banded together and formed the renegades of the Blackfoot Confederacy. They were waiting in their canoes camouflaged by the overhanging foliage from trees on the river's bank, knowing all too well that the steamboat would have to slow down to maneuver the river's bend. Once the steamboat blew the ship's whistle to slow down, the Indian parties boarded the steamboat killing the whole crew except for two hostages. The steamboat ran aground as the paddlewheel churned the muddy waters. The fate of the First Mate Johansson and Pilot Zimmermann were now in God's hands as they were carried off and disappeared into the river's mist.

Another warrant was issued to US Marshal Steve Zimmer to apprehend another gang but this one would be a little different! It seems that every generation gives birth to those with vigor for life; some have courage, others integrity with a will to do right and some good. But then there are those born to do squalor, the bad elements that degenerates to live in gangs and do harm. Notorious gangs sprung up throughout the west that plundered, murdered and robbed anybody or any establishment. Then scarce is that breed, angels in a time of need that bloom like a rare cactus rose in the desert.

There was such a gang known as the "filly avengers," a gang of all females that growing up were either mistreated or abandoned and wound up in an orphanage known as Our Lady of the Rosary. It was the only domicile that any of them knew. The orphanage struggled to make ends meet and once the girls became of age decided to band together and help the orphanage. The leader of the gang was "shoot 'em up" Jackie with her two six guns, and then there was June the Jaguar sleek and lean who moved like a cat. She liked to dance in the moonlight and blow up banks with her nitro. There was also Belinda from the east with her Henry Repeater which she enjoyed tremendously because she could load her rifle once on Sunday and shoot if off the rest of the week. Then there was Sharon from the Windy City with her two double barrel shotguns. She blasted four holes in everything! Finally, there was Deadeye Diane from the bayou who always carried three bowie knives. Two criss-crossed on her back so she could reach over her shoulders and pull them as quick as a wink and one between her legs. She always said that if a man can have his whopper between his legs, then she could carry a bowie knife between hers! Her claim to fame was she could hit a bull's eye every time from a hundred paces. She enjoyed throwing her boys, as she referred to her Bowie collection, and either part a man's hair or place one between his legs as most men would cringe and cup their family jewels in fear when they saw her in action.

But no matter what ever happens, every year on the anniversary of the Assumption the "filly avengers" left two satchels of cash on the door step of the orphanage and road off into the sunset to pull another heist.

Steve had it on good authority that the gang was hiding out in a small, sleepy town of Harmony Crossing in Arkansas just across the border from Louisiana. All their robberies were done at night when the banks were closed, so no one was ever hurt or killed. Steve wanted to be there before they rode out of town and covertly follow them before they made another fortunate heist. Upon the arrival in town of Harmony Crossing, the gang of female marauders were easy to locate for they stuck out like a cactus in the desert. Steve kept a low profile and patiently waited for their next move. They rode to a town of El Dorado, Arkansas, and waited for nightfall before robbing the bank and riding off. They rode back to Harmony Crossing and stayed quiet for a couple of weeks to watch clandestinely if there were any reactions to the robbery. Steve enjoyed watching their every move and chuckled to himself for this was not your typical outlaw gang. The entire group was quiet, reserve and extremely polite to others not to advert any attention to themselves as they went about their daily chores. Most gangs were hostile, boisterous, and troublesome, always ready for a gun fight. One morning Steve intentionally bumped into one of the girls just to see what would happen.

"Oh, excuse me, ma'am," Steve exclaimed as he continued, "for my clumsiness!"

The one referred to as June the Jaguar replied, "That is quite alright, sir."

"Can I buy you a cup of coffee to make up for my clumsiness?" Steve asked.

"No, thank you, I have some errands to run," June replied and quietly walked away.

Steve enjoyed watching her as she walked away for she did move like a sleek cat.

Within a few days, the entire gang bordered a stagecoach and headed for a small town where the orphanage was located. Steve inquired about the stagecoach's itinerary and followed on horseback about a half a day's journey behind. Upon arrival in the small town of only eight buildings, it was not difficult to locate the whereabouts of the gang. In fact it was more difficult to stay out of sight and inconspicuous. There was one hotel with the stagecoach depot inside, one saloon, a hardware and dry goods depot along with a restaurant and a stable with a blacksmith shop to one end of town. On the other end of town, there was a small church and a large white four story building that was the Our Lady of the Rosary Orphanage. A rarity of hospitality and kindness in these parts run by the nuns to inspire those less fortunate. Within two days, the entire gang again boarded a stagecoach and headed back to Harmony Crossing. Steve inquired at the orphanage about the place and asked about the young ladies carefully trying to avert any suspicions about them. He learned from the sisters how each of the girls grew up in the orphanage and upon leaving did well in business and manage to always help the sisters and orphanage with a welcome relief of donations. Steve thanked the sisters for their hospitality and then decided to head south while the stagecoach of ladies headed north. Steve figured that beauty, charm and hearts of gold is a rarity in life, and wouldn't interfere with their destiny, whatever it may be.

He rode hard all day and by nightfall decided to make camp when he saw the glow of a camp fire in the distance. He slowly rode up and yelled out towards the campsite, "Hello there, may I ride into your campsite?"

A crusty old voice replied, "By all means, company is welcomed!"

Riding into the camp, Steve said, "Coffee smells good!"

The crusty old guy said, "Well, climb down and have some."

"Thank you, sir, my name is Steve, Marshall Steve Zimmer."

"Well, pleasure to make your acquaintance Marshall Steve Zimmer; I'm Marshall Rooster Immel."

The two of them enjoyed some coffee, light conversation, and some corn dodgers followed by some good old corn liquor.

The following morning breakfast was a hot cup of coffee, and then the two of them had some serious conversation. Steve asked Rooster where he was heading.

"I'm after the Mielke Gang, big bad Mike and his gang of cut throats," as Rooster took out a poster to show Steve.

"I sure could use your help if you're inclined to give it?" Rooster asked.

"Well, that all depends," Steve hesitated to be obliging.

Rooster quickly asked, "Depends on what?"

Steve looked Rooster square in his eyes and asked, "Do you just shoot to kill or do you try to apprehend?"

Rooster quickly replied, "I always give them the chance to surrender or draw first! But if there is any foul play, I shoot to kill!"

Then Steve explained to Rooster the episode that happened at Pine Bluff.

"Yeah, I heard about that," Rooster said. "They were a mean bad bunch and I knew that the order came down from the top."

Rooster continued, "Well, Pilgrim, the only thing I can say is that the job was done for the right reason. Not necessarily the right way! Let juries decide if they're to be hung or not!"

With that answer, Steve felt obliged to help.

Rooster had been trailing the Mielke bunch for the past two weeks and had some inclination where they were heading. It seems they had a cabin up in the Blue Ouachita Mountains of Oklahoma. It would be another four-day ride before reaching their destination. But once they reached their destination, one could see the smoke rising from cabin's stove.

The cabin was backed into the side of the mountain with a small stream running in front of her. Rooster told Steve to cover the front left as he positioned himself to cover the right side of the cabin.

"I'll fire two shots in the air and ask them to surrender," Rooster whispered. "Be ready to comply with your Henry Repeater."

Before Rooster could even fire one shot, big Mike came out of the cabin, blasting away with his six guns and diving for cover behind some logs as three other hombres of his gang came out shooting their guns. Steve quickly returned fire with his Henry, killing one and fatally shooting another. Rooster with his shotgun got another.

Big Mike threw out his gun and yelled, "Enough, I surrender!"

Rooster yelled back, "Alright then, stand up, raise your arms, and walk towards us!"

Big Mike hesitated too long before standing so Rooster fired another barrel from his shotgun.

Big Mike shakily stood up and walked towards Rooster while Steve checked out the others.

"Any more in the cabin?" yelled Rooster.

"No, no more!" yelled Mike.

Steve yelled while checking the other three, "Two dead and one badly wounded."

Steve tried the best he could to patch the wounded guy up, but he died before nightfall.

"Well, you did the best you could Pilgrim but shotgun wounds are usually fatal," Rooster said as he patted Steve on the shoulder.

He continued, "Might as well make camp here for the evening, I'll tie Big Mike to that tree over yonder as you make a camp fire."

Steve questioned Rooster, "Why not camp in the cabin?"

Rooster replied, "I prefer the stars over my head to a rooftop, unless it's raining."

Steve got busy in making a fire and heating up some coffee.

After supper, the two of them got to chew the fat on life, outlaws and marshaling when Steve asked Rooster, "What are your plans now?"

"I reckon getting this guy to Fort Smith where Judge Josiah Potts and a jury can decide what to do with him," Rooster replied while sipping his coffee.

"What about you, Pilgrim, what's your next step?"

"I started this job with you, and I'll see it through to the end!" replied Steve.

"Good for you Pilgrim, glad to have the company," Rooster agreeably said.

At one point in their conversation the "filly avengers" was mentioned and Rooster said, "Yeah, I know of that bunch, beautiful lassies that ride together and I tell ya, that I had a fancy on their leader!"

"Well, what happened?" asked a quizzical Steve.

"Every time I got close to her, she would pull out her six guns," Rooster said.

At that comment they both had a good laugh and turned in for the night.

The next morning, they packed their gear, loaded the dead men on horses and tied off Mike on one big horse before heading down the trail and on to Fort Smith, Arkansas which was just a little north across the border from Oklahoma. Their progress was slow but made Fort Smith in four days. This Fort Smith always had a presiding judge and a scaffold was always up and ready for the next hanging. It didn't take long to get a jury together and have a trial. And as quickly as the trial was started, a verdict was reached of, "Guilty as hell!"

The following morning at 10 a.m. sharp, the deputies led out Big Mike and walked him up the gallows stairs.

The local sheriff asked the condemned man if he had any last words or request before the sentence was carried out.

Big Mike replied, "Nope, just one last bite and chew of tobaccee."

One of the deputies pulled out a big wad of tobacco and allowed Big Mike his final bite and watched him chew.

He then hurled the biggest, blackish, putrid spit over the railing of the gallows hitting one big lady on her flowery hat.

The judge, seeing that incident, bowed his head giving signal for the hangman to pull the lever sending Big Mike dangling through the trap door. His legs kept jumping and thrashing all over. Some say he danced all the way to hell!

Steve bid farewell to Rooster and headed off into the sunset back to New Orleans, not knowing what news was in store for him.

Meanwhile back on the Mighty Mississippi River, Wolfgang received word about his brother from the shipping company. Whenever one receives shocking, heart rendering news it jolts one's body to the very depth of the soul. Wolfgang upon his return to New Orleans went to see his brother Otto and break the news about their brother Kurt.

"Is there anyone trying to rescue him?" Otto asked as he did the sign of the cross.

Wolfgang replied, "No one knows if he is alive or dead!"

Otto, in complete disarray, went to the chapel to pray. When everything appears hopeless, there is only one person to turn to and seek His help and His comfort in prayer. Wolfgang followed his brother in silence.

Upon entering the church both walked up to the sanctuary and kneeled. Fr. Otto put on his stole and lifting his arms and outstretching them to God with tears streaming down his face, made this prayer:

"Behold, my beloved and good Jesus.
I cast myself upon my knees in your sight,
And with the most fervent desire of my soul,
I pray and beseech you to impress upon my heart,
Lively sentiments of faith, hope and charity,
With true repentance for my sins and a most firm desire of amendment;
While with deep affection and grief of soul I consider within myself and mentally contemplate your five most precious wounds,
having before my eyes that which David the prophet long ago spoke about you, my Jesus, they have pierced my hands and my feet; I can count all my bones!
God come to our assistance; Oh Lord, make haste to help our brother Kurt. Amen."

Both brothers left the church together knowing that Kurt's fate was in good hands from above!

Chapter 6
St. Lawrence Riverway

Uncle Allexander walked up to the podium and announced, "Ladies and gentlemen and distinguished guest, may I present to you our next Prime Minister of Canada and our future, Mr. John A. Macdonald."

Another era begins as John A. Macdonald walked up to the podium and announces his cabinet members along with Gustavus Bergstrom as minister of transportation and natural resources. The long haul to reestablish himself is finally ready to blossom and bear fruit. Wilhelm Axelson is his deputy chief and between the two of them progress is being made. Lucas has now graduated from the university with his law degree and passed the provincial bar examination and has gone to work for the distinguished law firm of Audet, Farnsworth, & LaPointe as an attorney. Throughout most of Canada the profession is known as barrister or solicitor but the term solicitor or *avoué*, never took hold in colonial Quebec. He has been learning the ropes and work-ing feverishly to excel to the level of barrister. His dad's advice to learn the jurisprudence of the law well is paying off. And having completed his internship he is indeed ac-quiring a passion for the law.

Wilhelm's son, Sebastian, also graduated from the uni-versity with an engineering degree and is working for the provincial energy department. His other sons, Oscar and Hugo, both have completed their apprenticeships at the shipyard with Oscar promoted to being a foreman and Hugo working in the drafting department.

It seemed that the newly elected conservatives who ran on a platform of protectionist tariffs were highly favored among the people. And now being newly elected and fully entrenched, the people wanted delivery on promises made which included a better economy, jobs and a completion of the transcontinental railway to the pacific coast.

Gus became buried in projects and his calendar full of appointments throughout the whole year. Whenever he got overwhelmed, Gus would sit back in his chair and stare at the picture on his desk of Svante, Olivia and their grandson Adam who is now five years old. Time has a way to slip by without notice like melting ice, one minute it is there, the next minute it is gone. But for him it was months slip-ping away into years. Now he had to refocus his mind and get ready for his meeting which is two days away in the national capital of Ottawa with the agenda for Canada's transportation issues, energy demands and utilization of natural resources. Along with each of these issues there were hurdles of legal problems of legislation to be passed, appropriations for funds, land issues and union grievances. Four different law firms, including Audet, Farnsworth, & LaPointe, were kept busy to keep abreast with the entire legal mumble jumble. A new hurdle arose as the demand for timber increased for railroad ties to finish the transcontinental railway. Wood, being the staple of Canadian trade for much of the 19th century fueled by European demand as well as Canadian priorities, brought much investment to Canada and fostered economic growth. The industry depended heavily on the muscles of men and beasts to fell, crosscut and drag logs to the rivers for transport to many sawmills where timber was prepared into planks and square timber. Some 3000 railroad ties made primarily from Douglas fir are needed to complete one mile of track. At one point William Price, "le pere du Saguenay," employed better than one thousand men and had sawmills at Chicoutimi along the Saguenay River. Apparently due to deplorable living conditions within the logging camps, loud uproars of a strike could be heard all the way to Quebec from Saguenay. All complaints and grievances wound up on the desk of Gustavus Bergstrom with the simple encouragement from the Prime Minister to, "Fix it, damn it!"

Problems surface as quickly as a bobber on a fishing line and accumulate like gnats swarming around your head.

No sooner had the threats surfaced about the logging strike, when a skirmish broke out in Saskatchewan over unfair encroachments by the government to take land by imminent domain for extending the railway to the Pacific Coast. The Métis People who settled the land and formed an ancestry from intermarriage between Indian women and European men didn't like the government taking their land ipso facto. Gus decided that the only way to get firsthand information was to go to Saguenay and end any notion of a strike. That left Wilhelm to travel to Saskatchewan and find out what the hell is going on and wire the information to Gus. This had to be accomplished in time for Gus to make his meeting in Ottawa in two days. Gus called in his staff and required that three things must be accomplished before he arrived in Saguenay. "First, contact the union and get a list of their grievances so I am not blindsided when we meet. Second, arrange a meeting so I can address all, and I do mean all involved, that means all loggers too!" Objections came from his staff that it could get rough with all present but Gus held up his hands and said, "I want all present."

He continued, "All concerned need to hear what I have to say!"

"Last, get the biggest tent that you can find and a hundred cases of the best whiskey there and set up before I finish my meeting with them."

One of his closest allies on his staff asked Gus, "What on earth are you going to say?"

Shaking his head Gus replied, "I don't have the faintest idea, but when I'm done, we'll all need a drink!"

With that said both Gus and Wilhelm shook hands and wished each other well and left for their destinations in opposite directions.

Upon arrival in Saguenay, Gus entered the huge meeting hall with close to a thousand people in attendance. The list of grievances was handed to Gus as he stopped, read each item on the list, shook his head in the affirmative and walked up to the podium. He began by saying, "Top of the evening! For those of you that know me, I am a straight shooter, and for those that don't, tonight you will learn that I am. You are the backbone of Canada! Because of your muscle and hard work, we will extend Canada to the west coast, bring new jobs to our economy and make Canada sing again! I have read your list of grievances and came here not to talk but to eliminate them. Starting tomorrow first thing new accommodations, better living conditions and better food will be available. Second, I understand that each of you work long, unforgiving hours. For every two weeks of work with rotated shifts each man will be allowed two days off with extra pay. There will be an open line to my office for any new grievances so that together we can settle them expeditiously. Merde est merde, translated in French, shit is shit, it doesn't matter if it's the Prime Minister's, mine, yours, a Yukon moose or a Klondike bear; I came to eliminate le merde! I am not much for long speeches so I ask you, are you with me or not?"

A tumultuous roar of cheers echoed throughout the hall.

With that Gus yelled, "Drinks are on the house! Let's adjourn to the tent!"

The strike was averted, Gus felt a sigh of relief and all one hundred cases of whiskey were consumed.

Upon his return to Quebec City there was a wire waiting for him from Wilhelm which read:

"Volatile situation stop
Some fighting stop
May need troops stop
See you in Quebec stop
Signed Wilhelm stop"

Not the best news to expect, but now Gus understood the gravity of the situation and waited for Wilhelm's' return for the rest of the story. Whenever something agitated Gus, he would occupy himself with another project to stay active, busy and sharp and never let the mind grow dull. He outlined his agenda for the meeting and was just about to put the finishing touches to his report when Wilhelm walked into the office.

Gus greeted him by saying, "Well, my friend, do we have to fight or not?"

Wilhelm, shaking his head, asked, "Have you ever heard of a Louis David Riel?"

Gus, scratching his head, replied, "It seems that I have heard of his name mentioned once or twice before but always in the negative or with some blasphemy behind it."

"Well," Wilhelm continued, "he is some political leader of the Métis people and founder of the province of Manitoba."

Gus, being very direct, said, "Go on; you have my full attention!"

"Back in 1869 to 70 he started some resistance known as the Red River Rebellion and he ordered the execution of some Protestant that annoyed him, a guy by the name of Thomas Scott. Apparently, he is some lunatic who thinks he has some divine calling and does anything he so pleases. But here lies the problem, the Métis people love him and consider him to be "Father of Manitoba. Now he resides in Saskatchewan, and trouble is brewing."

"Gus," Wilhelm continued, "this is a very touchy situation, a powder keg ready to explode!"

Gus agreed and asked Wilhelm to send a telegram.

"OK, to whom and what is the topic?" asked Wilhelm.

"Address it to Major General Patrick Smet of the RNWMP," which stood for Royal Northwest Mounted Police.

"Caution, Battle coming stop
Batoche Saskatchewan area stop
Culprit Louis David Riel stop
Best Regards
"And sign my name to it forth with."

"Now let's prepare for tomorrow's meeting and we can finish the report tonight on the train to Ottawa!"

Oh, the spectacular view of Ottawa built on a cluster of hills along the waterfront with sheer cliffs of limestone rising above the river. The Rideau Canal divides the city as it extends along a wide curve on the south bank of the Ottawa River which plunges some fifty feet or better in the turbulent Chaudière Falls as the Rideau River zigzags northward and drops some forty feet over the misty Rideau Falls. The natural beauty proves how God enjoyed carving out thee, as one's eyes scan the horizon to take it all in. Parliament Hill appears especially picturesque, grandiose with its monumental tower in the center of the façade and the balance of symmetry of gothic elements. Gus enjoyed the city of Ottawa almost as much as he enjoyed Quebec. But now both Gus and Wilhelm must ready themselves to sell both their ideas and ideals to parliament for the future of Canada.

Gus approached the Podium as Wilhelm sets up two large posters on the agenda for all in Parliament to see.

Gus adjusted the speaker and then began by saying, "Mr. Prime Minister, distinguished guest and members of parliament, we are about to embark into a new century. We need to be ready for the challenges of tomorrow. The farmer is always ready to set the plow to the earth and begin plowing and the soldier is always prepared to fight today to preserve tomorrow. We in parliament must set up the committees to direct our efforts and appropriate the funds to have the means to tap our resources in the areas of:

- Energy
- Forestry
- Water – Locks to accommodate larger ships and dams to generate our electricity
- Transportation by both Rail and Ship
- Mining – Tap all our natural resources
- Resource development and infrastructure
- Protection to Preserve – Form a Royal Mounted Police for all of Canada,"

As Gustavus continued, he had the undivided attention of all within Parliament. When Gus concluded his presentation, he was completely washed-out.

The train ride back to Quebec was a time for reflection, a couple of Jack Daniels and a relaxing smoke with the pipe as the scenery whirled by looking out the window. Snowflakes were dropping and Gus's mind floated back to a different time when the kids were growing up and he seemed to have more time to appreciate them. He had again achieved a certain status of success and now was gaining the momentum and power to see the enterprises come to fruition but was Gus happy? Time was quickly passing by and his mind floated in an out between reality and dreams. He thought about the innocents of youth to dream, the maturity of middle age to hope and now through the wisdom of old age to acquire some patience to understand and know that there are more precious things in life.

Wilhelm called out to Gus, "Gus, where are you?"

Coming back to reality, the thoughts faded about growing up and the life he once knew in Gavle for Gus was beginning to realize how much he missed his home town and the Old Country of Sweden.

Gus, shaking his head, looked upon his longtime friend and just asked for another drink.

The next few days were busy days indeed with delegating authority, setting up committees and keeping track of skirmishes in Saskatchewan but more importantly in talking with Elsa on making a trip to Maine to see family and friends. Elsa smiled and came alive when Gus mentioned a trip to Maine. The next day at the office Gus approached Uncle Allexander's office to break the news about the trip to Maine and ask if he and Clara would care to join them. As he stepped through the door Uncle Al was seated in his chair looking out the window with his back towards Gus.

Gus walked in and said, "Top of the morning, Uncle."

There was no response or even any movement as Gus got closer to the chair. He put his hand on Uncle Al's shoulder and still there was no movement. Gus looked down on his Uncle and the shock of reality settled in to find that his Uncle had passed on to eternal life. He bowed his head, said a short prayer and then made the proper arrangements and then went to see Clara.

The next few days were somber days with the funeral arrangements and making sure that Clara was alright. The tombstone read, "A Son of Canada," and then the years 1792-1890. He had lived a full life of ninety-eight years.

I don't exactly remember how the adage goes if work needs us or we need work, but Gus kept himself busy. Work does find a way to rob some of the precious moments in life. Just then his son Lucas walked into the office and was extremely perplexed about his pending case in court. He explained to his dad that the case of "The Providence of Manitoba vs. The Pacific Railroad in Land Rights" is a sticky issue.

Shaking his head in the affirmative Gus replied, "That's why we have lawyers!"

Gus, smiling at his son, continued, "Look son, the law is not only about being legal and right; it's also about putting it in the right context so that it is irrefutable!"

"Son, you have learned the law well, but you must also learn your audience and the knack of the argument to convince and persuade your point of view."

"Now how exactly do I do that?" Lucas asked.

"Come on son, that's basic law 101, you establish that in your opening comments!"

"Remember," his dad continued, "your opening comments needs to grab with the objective and then learn to use your objections at the right moment. Remember always punch and counter punch, and don't allow the defense to get the upper hand. It's just like a boxing match except without the blood!"

His son asked, "How hard does one have to punch?"

Gus, smiling, replied, "That all depends."

"Depends on what?" asked Lucas.

"It depends on how badly you want to win!" Gus replied.

"And that is just the way life is, life will throw you some punches and one needs to learn to counter punch, duck, or deck the opponent."

"Now," Gus added, "there is one more option that we learn in the Bible, to turn the other cheek, but that doesn't work in law. In law, you are either defending or attacking!"

In the pursuing months, Riel was called upon by the Métis leaders to be an advocate for their rights and trouble began to brew. As with most conflicts negotiations come to a standstill and Riel's followers seized arms, took hostages and cut the telegraph lines between Batoche and Battleford. The situation becoming critical called for drastic measures as the North-West Mounted Police were called upon to proceed from the north as a thousand troops were transported by train to Batoche where Riel and his men barricaded themselves to fight to the finish. Ensuing battles by the Métis Natives took place at Fort Carlton and at Duck Lake. As rebellion and chaos erupted, the prime minister wanted this conflict to be squashed with force. And by God it was swiftly done with Riel arrested along with other leaders and tried in a court of law. The prime minister ordered the trial to be convened in Regina where a jury found Riel guilty but recommended mercy; nonetheless, Judge Hugh Richardson sentenced him to death for treason where a white cap was pulled over his face and he was hung. In the pursuing months, as public sentiment mellowed, Riel's tombstone was erected at the St. Boniface Cathedral.

The long-awaited vacation and trip to Maine finally arrived, not exactly the way Gus had planned it but with his wife Elsa at his side the trip by train was both scenic and peaceful. Lucas was up to his armpits in legal matters, Wilhelm had to attend to business and Clara didn't want to make the trip without her husband. Life does move on but sometimes woe is me as the saying goes.

By now the foundry in Bath had expanded twice and in 1888 acquired a shipbuilding company and was doing well. By 1890, they were ready to launch their first steamer. Both Hjalmar and Svante were doing well within the business and when Gus placed an order for four more ships, the champagne was uncorked to celebrate. Gus had sold his rights of the Bath Maritime Trust to his son some previous years ago, so not to conflict with Canadian politics. The only thing left was to enjoy family and friends and play with his grandson Adam.

Every nation has that faction of society that crawls out from the gutter to do no good and leave a foul stench like from a septic tank freshly opened after a long winter. And with such deficient immigration laws of Canada, there was more to organized crime in Canada than the Italian criminal gang known as the "Mob." It was far easier to immigrate into Canada then the United States and set up shop along with bribing magistrates, law enforcement, and barristers. Parliament had defined in the criminal code of Canada organized crime as a group of three or more people whose purpose is the commission of one or more serious offences that would likely result in the direct or indirect receipt of a material benefit, including a financial benefit, by the group. What a bunch of legal mumble jumble. A more succinct definition was given by a former mob boss as "just a bunch of guys getting together to take all the money they can from all the suckers they can!"

It all started out so unobtrusively in the transportation business of imports and exports with booze, weapons, like those shipped to the Métis Natives, services of protection and other goods along with gambling. One day a tall, lean thug walked into the provincial parliament building of Quebec and meandered his way to Gus's office. Placing a large satchel of money upon his desk, he spoke with indifference on how each of their businesses could benefit each other. Gus stood up from his desk, opened the satchel and saw the large sum of money and surmised a bribery if there ever was one and opened his desk drawer, pulled out a loaded revolver and shot the bastard wounding him in the shoulder. The authorities who stood guard at the parliament building upon hearing the gun shots, rushed up the stairs and into the minister's office. The blasphemous intruder was spewing all types of obscenity from his mouth so Gus shot him again and demanded he shut up or you will be dead. Gus was never a push over and demanded to lock up the culprit in containment of the local authorities and barked at his associate to get Major General Patrick Smet immediately!

A wire was issued to the NWMP to the attention of Major General Patrick Smet to come to Quebec at once and interrogate this bastard.

Another wire was sent to Prime Minister Macdonald about this incident and the possibility of organized crime in Canada recommending a joint emergency meeting of the cabinet and parliament.

Within 24 hours, a prompt Major General Patrick Smet arrived in Quebec with twenty men and had a subpoena to release the culprit over to the NWMP. They escorted him to a place of his choosing, a hockey rink, for a favorite pastime sport in Canada is hockey and it is now midnight in mid-January. The major general had his men suit up along with their ice skates. Each man was given these specially made huge paddles versus the traditional hockey sticks and the culprit was dragged upon the ice, stripped naked and unofficially became their hockey puck. The major general blew his whistle and that poor bastard was battered all over the ice before he confessed his guts out as to names, places and associates within the organization that became known as the "Quebec Quagmire." A list to what the culprit confessed was made with every "i" dotted and every "t" crossed. Once all the necessary information was gathered, the three musketeers of Canada, Gus, Wilhelm and the major general proceeded to Ottawa. The emergency joint session of the cabinet and parliament was called to order as the proclamation on organized crime and gangs was read. News of the emergency joint session was leaked to the media and an overwhelming outcry from the public wanted Parliament to enact stronger, more stringent laws against organized crime and gangs. Gus felt good because he has been demanding a Royal Mounties Police Force for some time now. In the interim, Major General Patrick Smet was put in charge of a special group known as the Shotgun Mounties. Each man was handpicked and especially trained with four barrel shotguns. One by one all providences got a Special Forces unit and Parliament passed the necessary legislative laws to combat this injustice. The Criminal Code of Gangs Act which stated that no matter how many members in the gang, if one culprit of said gang commits a crime then all said members of the gang are guilty because the purpose of the gang is to harbor crime. There was one additional clause that impacted organized crime where it stated any crime committed that involves a killing, the said culprits do not have to be apprehended but shot dead. After that organized crime and gangs moved to Chicago and New York.

The drastic measures enacted in Canada had much fallout from the United States and from a President Benjamin Harrison who thanked the prime minister all to hell for sending all the crime bosses to America. This forced the United States to enact laws and tighter regulation on immigration by opening Ellis Island in New York Bay in 1892 and having a direct telephone line between the Prime Minister and President thanks to the efforts of Alexander Graham Bell, long distance was made possible and swearing on line could be live versus sending a wire!

The crime bosses might have fled to America but there was an ominous cloud hanging over Gus as he addressed other issues for Canada. Violent crime can shatter lives and families, and it always remains a factor where people choose to live, worship and work. It always remains a potent political issue that calls for social reform as well as "law and order." The whys and wherefores of life are never easy to answer without prayer and guidance from above.

The transcontinental railway had been completed connecting all providences from east to west but the problem of transporting goods and supplies north and south was still a huge problem. One of the world's two most important food crops is wheat, and the other is rice. On the prairies of Canada conditions exist that are ideal for growing hard spring wheat which is their leading crop and main export. And again, as usual the prime minister turns to Gustavus as problems in his domain surface to "Fix it."

The prairie levels of western Canada produce abundant yields of wheat throughout the providences of Alberta, Saskatchewan and Manitoba, and as usual as we try to solve our problems, we create many more. Throughout the great era of wheat growing many inventions sprung up beginning with Cyrus McCormick's new reaper enabling farmers to grow far more wheat with the same man power. This was followed by new ways to plant and harvest the crop but without the necessary trains or ships to transport the wheat a colossal standstill erupted between production and transportation.

Gus' solution to the whole problem was to privatize the railroad in each providence with entrepreneurs to financially back the construction and extend the rail and leave the weightier problems of shipping to his department. With the entrance of other countries into the wheat trade, the wheat shipping business grew up around the world. Liverpool, England, strategically located for trading, became a world power in controlling prices. Chicago and Winnipeg also developed as world trading centers. Again, Gustavus rolled up his sleeves as he and Wilhelm engineered solutions to handle all the shipments. And as always there were miles of legal hurdles to eliminate that kept the legal teams busy as the years passed.

The demand for timber soared as each providence competed to extend the railroad and transporting cost from the east became prohibitive as the center for Canadian wood production gradually shifted westward. British Columbia overnight saw logging camps and sawmills spring up like a blooming valley. Lumbering on the rugged West Coast required considerable adaptation from the eastern techniques. Three times as many oxen were required to pull their loads and skid roads had to be built of logs. With the larger trees, cuts were made higher on the huge trunks which required a springboard for each of the two axmen to stand on using double-bitted axes. And again, grievances and complaints erupted from the logging camps and sawmills of Dobbler, Kingston, and Hornsby. This time Gus decided to travel and meet the owners at a halfway point between Vancouver and Quebec. Both parties agreed to meet in Winnipeg which was a big mistake on Gus's part. The Métis People of both Manitoba and Saskatchewan never forgave the Canadian government for the death of their fearless leader Louis David Riel. Rumors spread quickly like a forest fire in strong winds as news circulated about the big meeting in Winnipeg. Organized crime from Chicago also got wind of the meeting and figured this would be an opportune time to settle an old score.

Preparations were made for his trip to Winnipeg and again Gus asked for a list of grievances. Upon receiving the list Gus noticed that the complaints weren't about the back-breaking work but the fatality rate of handling the stubborn oxen and transporting the large logs. Calling in Wilhelm and other associates for an emergency meeting to go over each item, Gus asked for three things.

There was an innovation invented in the United States known as the steam-powered donkey which could drag logs many miles versus the traditional usage of oxen. And then another innovation known as the "high lead system," in which a line high over the skids lifted logs over obstacles in the forest. Both items would reduce substantially injuries and fatalities. The third item was an insurance policy for each worker for hospital care and life insurance for the surviving families which till now was unheard of. Gus knew all too well the rigors of life and of loss. Gus directed Wilhelm to find information on cost, point of purchase, availability of units and if they could ship to Vancouver. Next his associate got bids on needed insurance policies to forward to Dobbler, Kingston, and Hornsby. Gus was determined to avert any work stoppage at all cost. The meeting having been finalized for Winnipeg and with all contingencies in place to cover each of the grievances, Gus got ready for the long train ride. Unaware that Wilhelm had conversations with Major General Patrick Smet, there would also be twelve plain clothes men traveling on the train who were sworn to uphold law and order and to protect Gustavus Bergstrom at all cost.

Gustavus stepped onto the train to board for his three-day journey. He carried along the good book for some Bible reading because taking the time for daily prayer and reflection was a ritual with Gus from his boyhood days. Then there was a bottle of Jack Daniels, his companion on many a lonely night. The train pulled away from the Quebec Depot and from his window he gazed upon this country known as the land of the maple leaf. The second largest nation in the world Canada is twenty-two times the size of Sweden. Gus couldn't help but compare his homeland to this vast country and tried to fathom the broadness of this huge land. Over the next three days he sat back and took in the panoramic views of the regions as he passed through what was known as the Canadian Shield or Laurentian Plateau which covers some 1,850,000 square miles or about half the total area of Canada. Gus had lived here now for better than fifteen years and was just beginning to appreciate the beauty and vastness of this great nation of five natural regions.

There was little fanfare for his arrival into Winnipeg, the conglomerate of Dobbler, Kingston and Hornsby had made all arrangements for Gus to be chauffeured to one of the better hotels where a conference room was utilized for the meeting. Essentially the meeting was cordial and highly productive with six units ordered of the steam-powered donkeys and high lead systems for each of the six logging camps. Some of the legal loop holes for the insurance policies had to be hammered out but both parties agreed to leave that to the attorney's legal mumble jumble. Resting assured that all bases were covered; the group enjoyed a scrumptious dinner, some cordial drinks and light conversation.

The next morning as Gus rode down in the elevator feeling good at the outcome of the meeting and ready to enjoy a hearty breakfast, gun shots ricocheted throughout the lobby as the elevator doors opened. Two gunmen across from the elevators came out blasting with Tommy guns. But the unexpected plainclothes men were on station and ready as they counter fired killing two of the culprits. A third gunman came out from the newsstand and shot Gus in the back as he ducked and turned the corner from the elevator. That bastard was quickly wounded and apprehended but not before the downfall of Gus. Sometimes the best conceived plans are not good enough as they rushed Gus to the hospital.

Chapter 7
The Legend of FT

The headlines on the New Orleans Gazette read, "Homestead Massacre," seven guards and eleven strikers shot to death July 6, 1892. Workers at the Carnegie Steel Mill in Pennsylvania clash with security guards. The following Sunday Father Otto gave the sermon and the first reading hit home in lieu of all that had transpired with the recent massacre, receiving a letter from his brother Axel that mater had died and still not knowing the status of his brother Kurt. The words became lucid and penetrated to the very heart of his soul as the reading proceeded from the Book of Job, "Remember: life is a breath; I will vanish from your sight. The eye that looks will not see me; you may search but I will be gone. Like a cloud fading in the sky, man dissolves into death. And never comes home again."

After the readings, Fr. Otto gave his homily as he began by saying, "My dear friends in Christ, everyone has heard of Ralph Waldo Emerson who was also a preacher as well as an essayist. He once preached that each human being has a spark of divinity in them which gives you power. Not Almighty Power, not power of might but the power to discern to know and to do right. As we go through life all of us experience pain and in that pain, know to turn to God in prayer and in our supplications, earnest prayer helps purify our soul. We turn to God because he is the higher cause of all things; He is our Almighty Father who sent his son to show us the way and to teach us to also be obedient unto death. The commandments and beatitudes teach us how to live and He gave us His only son who died for each one of us! And so, I ask each one of you now, how can anyone want to cheat life but more importantly cheat God who is our Heavenly Father?"

Fr. Otto has been a priest serving God, his holy church and growing flock for some eighteen years now. And during that time, he never personally asked for anything for himself from above except for true guidance and a true spirit to serve. Last night he prayed with his whole heart for a sign to know if his brother Kurt was alive or dead. It has now been a tormenting thirteen years and no closure on the chapter of his brother's life. When he talked to the Bishop about his feelings, he would encourage Fr. Otto to pray for the forbearance of our Holy Mother Mary who had the strength, forbearance and patience to watch her son die and yet see the glory of his resurrection.

Wolfgang was still a pilot on the mighty Mississippi River and was enjoying a brew in the "Devil's Den Saloon" when a huge fur trapper walked up to him and asked, "Say, are you pilot Wolfgang Zimmermann?"

Giving an acknowledgement the trapper handed Wolfgang a smooth polished stone. Looking a little bewildered the trapper told him to turn it over. Upon turning the stone over, he found an inscription that read, "I'm fine, Brother Kurt."

Upon asking the trapper to explain where on earth he got this stone, Wolfgang ordered a drink for his new-found friend and had him sit down to retell his story. It seems that he was trapping high in the mountains of Montana when he came upon a small tribal village of the Piegan, Blackfoot. Among the tribe there was this one white man with an Indian squaw and two little braves. He gave me this stone and told me to look up a pilot Wolfgang Zimmermann and personally hand him this stone. He told me that you would know what to do with it. Wolfgang at this point didn't know whether to shout with joy or cry but ordered another round of drinks for them both. The trapper's name was Big John Dawson six foot seven and close to 380 lbs. Didn't ride a horse because the last one he rode died of pure exhaustion, so he walked and trapped for a living. Before their departure Big John drew a map to where he could find his brother. Wolfgang thanked him kindly and grasped the stone with his brother's signature and couldn't believe his eyes as he stared at the stone that his brother was still alive.

The day of his capture the two hostages were taken to the Blackfoot Forest through Moccasin Pass that wound around Buffalo Rock Mountain to the Indian camp on Eagle Lake. High in the mountains where Spirit Twin Falls split over a huge boulder that looked like a buffalo head. The Indian camp of some 200 tipis spread out below the mountains to the southeast of Eagle Lake. In the center of the compound to where they were led there was a larger tipi where the tribal council met and ceremonies performed. Four huge poles stuck out from the ground about fifty paces from the tipi council, and both Johansson and Zimmermann were tied off at the stakes. The Indians truly believed that all white men spoke with fork tongues because most of the white men that they met were cutthroat, soldiers or just plain bad men who usually killed an Indian on sight. There was a short ceremony, an Indian dance performed by their shaman or medicine man seeking the Spirits council to decide the fate of these two men. Then four braves came out and joined in the dance with the holy man. The drum beats stopped signaling for the four braves to build a camp fire and placed two hunting knives of eight inch blades into the fire. Johansson turned to Kurt and just closed his eyes as the fear seized him, but Kurt raised his head and prayed to God to give him strength and let His will be done. With the blazing hot knives, the braves walked up to the hostages and held back their heads and since all white men speak with fork tongues, pulled out their tongues and split them with the hot blazing blades which cauterize them with a searing smell. Johansson screamed out an ungodly yell and then collapsed, but Zimmermann didn't utter a sound as he looked up towards heaven and prayed. Both the Indian Chief and Shaman took note of Kurt and admired his courage. Once Johansson regained his consciousness, he was untied and then a lance was hurled through the air and the Indian braves signaled for him to run. Kurt tried to give him some encouragement to keep the faith but now his words weren't clear as he spoke with a lisp. Johansson slowly started to run and once he passed the lance, the four braves followed in pursuit. The four braves quickly overtook and overpowered the First Mate and bludgeoned him to death with their tomahawks.

Now it was Kurt's turn to run the "race of the lance," as it was known amongst the Indian tribes. As the Indian braves untied his hands from the stakes, he raised his arms to heaven and prayed. Then as another lance was hurled through the air, Kurt was thinking about his strategy. He thought to himself, *Where on earth could I run to for I don't know these forests?* His only chance or hope was to stand his ground and fight to the end. He slowly ran to the lance and then stopped and turned to pull the lance out of the ground. Taking the lance and holding it high over his head to show the other braves that he wasn't afraid of them, he smashed the lance over his knee breaking it in two. Now he had two clubs and turned to face the charging braves ready to do battle. Kurt had learned as a pilot on the river to brawl and keep your opponents at bay. The Indian braves were getting closer as Kurt charged them giving out a loud war chant that startled them to stop long enough so he could disarm two of the braves and take on the foursome. He singlehandedly fought off each one by crisscrossing his clubs to avoid a tomahawk from splitting his head. Then one by one, overpowered each brave knocking them to the ground, but he would not kill them. The four battered braves dejectedly walked back to their camp. The chief sent four more braves to attack Kurt and again he defeated all four braves. Now Kurt held his two clubs high and gave out a mighty victory call. The test of battle went well into the night and at midnight the Indian tribe's chief, Brave Hawk, halted the test, for he did not want to offend the spirits. That night Kurt proved to the Blackfeet and to himself that he was indeed the bravest of all braves. From that night, the legend of "FT" became known throughout the Indian nations and circulated throughout the west. Songs were sung about the legend of FT.

"There once was a man who traveled the west,
Who met his fate in an Indian test.
A lance to outrun and no place to go,
He stood his ground and this I know.
His courage was great and his will was strong,
Along with his great strength the test lasted the day long.

He first fought off one and then another,

His fighting and courage couldn't be any better.

He fought through the night; defeat would not come in sight,

As he fought off the whole tribe, this battle became a bit trite.

This legend came to be for this fight was no little trifle,

From east to west, oh how he wished he had a rifle.

Now this legend continues from coast to coast,

About this Indian Test to win he can boast.

Keep courage and faith and you will overcome,

Any test in life with God can be won."

From that day forth Kurt became known as a brave warrior with the symbol of a bear tattooed on his right shoulder for he fought like a grizzly bear and was accepted into the tribe. As the seasons passed he learned of the Blackfoot ways, tongue and customs and in due time fell in love with a young Indian maiden known as "Song Bird," for the sound of her voice was as sweet as any song bird. The Indians had no written records, the maintenance of their historical accounts depended on the oral traditions. Each tribe had its elders who knew that it was their sacred duty to instruct selected young men carefully in their rich traditions of the nation. Kurt learned, enjoyed and fell in love with both an Indian maiden and the Indian nation. And through the years became a proud dad of two young braves known

as Spotted Owl and Red Wolf. Spotted Owl was wise for
his years and Red Wolf was cunning in all his deeds. Kurt
learned the native tongue well although with his speech impediment due to his split tongue became frank in his words.
But he was happy and enjoyed all that life had to offer for
in both worlds whether white or Indian, life is what you
make of it.

Wolfgang returned to his home port of New Orleans and
once the steamship was securely docked proceeded forth-
with to see his brother Otto and tell him of the joyous news
about their long-lost brother. Upon showing Fr. Otto the
polish stone with the inscription engraved on it, he blessed
God for his prayers have been answered. It indeed has been
a long absence of his brother and now he is found.

The following Sunday Fr. Otto began the Ordinary of
the Mass in the usual way,

"In Nomine Patris, et Filii, et Spiritus Sancti, Amen
Introibo ad altare Dei.
Ad Deum qui Iaetificat juventutem meam."

This in Latin means, "In the Name of the Father, and of
the Son, and of the Holy Spirit. Amen. I will go in to the
altar of God. The God of my gladness and joy."

Fr. Otto reflected to himself as he recited the mass in
Latin that someday in the wisdom from above, the church
will recite the mass in the vernacular of the people.

After mass Fr. Otto proceeded to see the Bishop. With
some eighteen years of service, he never once asked for a

vacation even though two weeks were permitted each year for some relaxation. His request upset the Bishop at first but once Fr. Otto showed His Holiness the polish stone from his brother with the inscription on the back side he quickly calmed down and wasn't so perplexed. He only asked, "Are you sure my son that you want to do this?"

Once Fr. Otto agreed, he received the Bishop's permission and blessing to, "Go in peace!"

Plans were set in motion for Fr. Otto, with the help from his brother Wolfgang, to travel by steamship to St. Louis and then change steamships and proceed up the Missouri River to Fort Benton. From there arrangements were made for trapper Big John Dawson to bring Fr. Otto to the Blackfoot Nation. With some thirty-six weeks of vacation time, Fr. Otto felt he had the time to find his lost brother and never gave any thought to the pending dangers that awaited him.

It is spring a good time to be traveling with the winter snows melting and the crisp fresh air blowing from the west. Passing many cities and rivers whose names I am not familiar with except for a few mentioned in the past by pilots Kurt and Wolfgang my brothers, souls in a brave new world not knowing what lies ahead in every bend of life. First there is Natchez, Grand Gulf, Vicksburg, Greenville, on to Memphis and then St. Louis busy ports of activity and plenty of time for prayer, reflection and reading my bible. The waters are swift with the spring thaw overflowing her banks here and there and the fresh blossoms scenting the air with birds returning north and the sun peaking higher in the sky. Do any of us take the time to appreciate God's creation, admire her beauty, and say thank you? The gift of life which is marvelous, enchanting and beyond our total comprehension to appreciate her fully is like the river that never stops flowing. A few drops of water can quench a thirst, baptize a newborn, or flow together in a torrential flood. There is still much snow along the banks of the muddy Missouri River, more hardwood trees and fewer towns as we glide along only seeing a trapper now and then or a band of braves bringing home freshly caught game. The ships whistle is now my time piece alerting to every trading post and bend in the river to maneuver. With a mighty blast on the ship's whistle, Fort Benton comes into view; it has been eight weeks of travel since leaving New Orleans. A crude looking outpost built in a quadrangle over 150 feet square with 25 foot square bastions and portholes in the bastion walls for both cannon and rifle to take aim if needed to defend the establishment. A large timbered gate was located between the northeast bastion and huge warehouse for all to pass and a smaller gate admitted Indians, a few at a time, into the enclosure where they could trade their furs and pelts for goods in return. Three flags on three poles waving in the wind, one Canadian, American and white flag to signal all are welcomed. Being close to the Canadian border many mountain men, explorers, fur traders, and thieves crossed over from both sides. Some years ago, the original site of the fort was further south but moved at the request from the Blackfeet over some sacred Indian ground dispute. Fort Benton is one of the most historically significant sites in Montana for as a trading post, military fort, and last depot for steamboat navigation; it also became an overland cross-roads connection from east to west and northward through the Whoop-up Trail from Fort Benton to Alberta, Canada. Fort Benton was also a supply station for the North West Mounted Police charged with bringing law and order to the wild, whiskey bastards of the western provinces. Their motto of "we get our man" meant to zigzag across the border at times. Between the keel boat thugs, hooligans, thieves and trappers there were many drunkard brawls at the Fort and a short walk to the stockade. Home if you could call it that for many of the lost souls of the west and for a few gentle souls such as Big John Dawson who was a courteous, kindly man who very seldom got roused but when he did, it took twenty able men to restrain him. As Fr. Otto walked into the tavern, all eyes gazed upon him for a priest was a rarity in these parts. Big John stood up and introduced himself to the padre and then sat down at his table.

"It's a bit of a journey Padre to the Blackfeet Nation," Big John began to say. "I took the option to get you a mule for the long trek up the mountains."

Fr. Otto, reflecting to himself how fitting for Jesus entered Jerusalem on a donkey, replied to Big John, "That will be fine."

The next morning their two-week trek began and gave time for each of the men to get to know each other. First thing each morning Fr. Otto would rise and say a Mass which Big John enjoyed and missed since his early days of being raised a Catholic. Both of his folks were killed in an Indian raid heading west and Big John had to fend for himself for many years now. He wasn't quite sure how old he was but looked between the years of 25 to 30 years old. A huge, strapping size man that enjoyed life and all its blessings. He was seven years old when his parents were killed and raised by the tavern keeper at Ft. Benton, hence reason for his fondness of the place. The odd friendship grew between them and they enjoyed each other's company, primarily because Fr. Otto would listen to Big John and talk with him without being bias of his size.

Looking up Fr. Otto admired the spectacular view of twin falls indicating that the Indian camp was near. As Big John led the donkey into the camp with Fr. Otto riding high, there was much chanting and waving from the crowd as they approached the Indian Chief and medicine man. Fr. Otto got off his mule and graciously bowed to the chief and then to his right noticed his brother Kurt standing with a smile from one ear to another. The brothers walked up to each other and embraced as tears streamed down the face of Fr. Otto, a sight unseen among Indian braves. It was a joyous meeting and as the day progressed from introductions from the chief on down through the tribe, Fr. Otto finally met Kurt's wife and children Spotted Owl and Red Wolf who are now seven and five years old. Fr. Otto got on his knees to greet the boys which was a new experience for them to meet their Uncle Otto or "Un'kl-O," as he became known to his nephews. Kurt didn't say much to his brother to hide his impediment but pointed and said only one word syllables until evening when the two were alone to talk and then the whole story was revealed about the legend of FT. At first Fr. Otto was horrified for his brother but quickly saw the happiness of the family and realized that the matter was irrelevant for any more questions.

As the days progressed into weeks, Fr. Otto began to pick up on the Blackfoot language which was part of the Algonkian dialect and learn more of their customs and traditions. Each morning he would rise early from his tipi and proceed to the cliff to say his morning prayers and offer daily sacrifice. And each morning the medicine man would rise and give chant and prayers as well. Their acquaintance grew and in due time the medicine man acquiesce to celebrate side by side with Ft. Otto as they climbed the mountain together and raising their arms to heaven recited a prayer:

Medicine-man	*Priest*
O Great Spirit	Our Father who art in heaven
Whose voice I hear in the winds	Hallow be thy name
Whose breath gives life to all the world	thy kingdom come; thy will be done

I need your strength and wisdom	on earth as in heaven
Let me walk in beauty, my eyes see the sunset	Give us this day our daily bread;
Make my hands respect what you have made	and forgive us our trespasses
Make me wise to understand you	as we forgive those who tres pass against us
Let me learn the lessons in every leaf and rock	and lead us not into temptation
I seek strength, not to be greater than others	but deliver us from evil.
Make me always ready to come to you	For the kingdom, the power and the glory
With my spirit without shame.	Are yours, now and forever.
Anistiopi	Amen

All nations throughout history and their development have committed some atrocities, but the greatest American Tragedy is how we treated the American Native. We stripped these beautiful people of their land, their rights and dignity and even of their traditions. Fr. Otto fell in love with these people, with their customs, rituals and glorious spirit.

There were many questions that Fr. Otto wanted to ask the Holy Man, White Eagle, the tribe's medicine man or shaman but answers were not available to outsiders because the oral tradition to recite them is sacred. One night "White Eagle" which stood for purity from the word white and able to see through the light from the word eagle invited Fr. Otto to his tipi. The eagle is the only animal that can look straight into the sun without being blinded. An amazing fact is that the Christian Religion has also given the symbol of the eagle to St. John of the fourth gospel because he could see the light of Christ's divinity. Three events had to occur before the holy man could reveal any of the Blackfoot traditions. The first was to smoke the spirit pipe or calumet to have a vision. If there is no vision, then the smoker of the pipe is not worthy. Once a vision is revealed then a ceremonial dance will follow to begin the spiritual quest. Once all three requirements of Pipe and Vision, Ceremonial Dance, and Spiritual Quest are met then and only then the two will become blood brothers and White Eagle will reveal some of the traditions of the tribe.

A custom of admitting an outsider to the tribe is a serious matter never to be taken lightly. A quorum of twelve members of the tribe had to be present at smoking of the pipe to witness the vision. Then after successfully completing all three requirements, the candidate will be presented before the whole tribe to be accepted or not. Present at the medicine man's tipi were seven of the tribal elders, Chief Brave Hawk, Holy man White Eagle and two brave warriors, one of them being Running Bear his brother. The twelfth person is Fr. Otto to complete the circle. Numerology was as important in the Indian traditions as well as the Jewish traditions as the number twelve signified a completion as the twelve tribes of Israel or the twelve apostles of Christ.

White Eagle prepared the tobacco for the pipe and then prepares the pipe for the ritual. Raising the pipe, he extended the stem of the pipe skyward to the Great White Spirit and then pointed the pipe towards the ground to mother earth. Holding the pipe ever so reverently, he then turned to the direction of the four winds to point the pipe first east, south, west, and finally north. The pipe stem is considered the connecting link to the supernatural and the smoke rising from the pipe would rise to the heavens to the Great White Spirit. Fr. Otto was indeed intrigued and respectful of the ceremony for in the Catholic Church, the thurible, or censer, is used filled with incense to symbolize that the rising smoke like our prayers rise to heaven. White Eagle, invoking wisdom from the Great Spirit, took four long puffs on the pipe and hands the pipe next to Brave Hawk seated to his left and the pipe was continually passed around the circle in the direction of the traveling sun with Fr. Otto receiving the pipe last. White Eagle, slowly blowing out his last puff, used both of his hands to fan the smoke to his face. Fr. Otto followed the practice and did the same. The pipe was passed back and forth seven times signifying the seven days of creation. At first Fr. Otto was startled as a vision comes into focus of many floating spheres rising to heaven. Then he heard much sobbing and found it very disturbing for he wasn't sure what the vision was about. They remained seated with their legs crisscrossed for what seemed to be a very long time. Once the vision cleared,

White Eagle, with the aid of Running Bear, interpreted the vision to Fr. Otto.

"Many seasons ago your federal government forced the relocation of five Native American tribes from their homelands to the designated 'Indian Territory' west of the Mississippi River. The Choctaw, Seminole, Creek, Chickasaw and the Cherokee were forced on a challenging and deadly journey known as the Trail of Tears. It was 2,200 treacherous miles expanding through nine states. More than 13,000 Native Americans lost their lives due to extreme weather conditions, disease and starvation. What the Great White Spirit allowed you to see and hear tonight were their sobs of tears and souls floating to heaven."

Fr. Otto, upon hearing this, could not compose himself any longer but wept deeply for this was too much to bear. All tribal members that were present witness not only the vision but the genuine grief of Fr. Otto and were moved.

The ceremony of visions was indeed an emotional draining event and so Fr. Otto could return to his tipi and sleep for tomorrow he would rise early for the ceremonial dance.

Sunrise peeked over the horizon as a proud White Eagle led the procession of elders to Fr. Otto's tipi. He was abruptly awoken and given a loincloth known as a breechclout to put on and thrust off his buffalo hide with the enthusiasm of giddy school children. The procession led a bewildered Fr. Otto as White Eagle tried to explain how to jump twice on each foot as one swayed from side to side raising one arm to heaven and the other down to mother earth at the same time to the drum beat. To begin the dance, raise both arms to heaven to thank the Great White Spirit and then alternate your arms with your knees and go to the drum beat.

The entire tribe was present to watch the debut of Fr. Otto as he stepped forward in his breechclout. His brother Running Bear along with his wife, Song Bird and their two children were there to watch and cheer Un'kl O on this sacred ceremony. Chief Brave Hawk stepped forward raises both hands to signal both White Eagle and Fr. Otto to step forward. Raising his voice for all to hear that it was a successful vision quest and that now and forever Fr. Otto will be known as "Spirit Heart" throughout the tribe and then Brave Hawk nodded to start the drum beats. White Eagle stepped forward and led Spirit Heart in cadence to encourage him on. Spirit Heart, always a humble man in prayer, gladly raised both of his hands toward heaven and, proud to be a member of the Blackfeet, stepped lively to the drum beat and got caught up in the spiritual dance. The entire tribe was ecstatic as Spirit Heart glided through the air in a circle always acknowledging first the Great White Spirit and then mother earth. After the ceremonial dance, he was greeted by all the tribe.

A feast followed with roasting of buffalo and elk meat as the main course and then Spirit Heart feeling like a little kid playing outside for the first time asked his nephews' what they wanted to do next. Their response, like most normal youngsters, was to go swimming and off they raced to Eagle Lake jumping in and making a big splash. Spirit Heart enjoyed the loose comfortable feeling of the breechclout, it was the original "crouch, without the ouch" unless you backed into a thorn bush, then Lord have mercy! It was an enjoyable time for all especially Spirit Heart and his nephews.

That night White Eagle, with a procession of elders came to Spirit Heart's tipi to prepare him for the spiritual quest that would last three days and three nights. He was led to the top of the mountain where he would seek and pray for three days throughout the elements of nature. Fr. Otto was used of keeping the vigil but not for three days. Indeed, this would be a test of his endurance and faith but knew that through God he would persevere. White Eagle looked intently into his eyes and with both hands motioned to Spirit Heart to look up towards the Great White Spirit by saying, "Ah-badt-dadt-deah" which means "the one who made all things." They left with him a water skin so he could drink a little water but no food, for this spiritual quest is their test of faith.

Spirit Heart watched the holy man and elders proceed back to their camp and then raising his hands to heaven began the spiritual quest. It doesn't matter which religion is practiced all faith is one in God and that poignant moment when it is just God and you, the human spirit is raised to enlightenment through His love and the communion is consummated. Too many people do not know how to speak to God or pray; they simply recite words. Therefore, the Father sent His son to show us the way and then to die for each one of us! As the Father, has given witness to us, we are to give witness to Him.

Before Spirit Heart realized it, White Eagle was touching his shoulders to retrieve him back to camp. He had completed the three-day spiritual quest. He was a little sore from a few blisters on his shoulders due to the hot sun but all in all in good spirits.

Throughout the next few weeks Spirit Heart observed, listened, and learned of the Indians' ways. There is a rhythm to their life as there is supposed to be in our life. They are spiritual centered; are we God centered? The main difference between the Indian and the Christian is that they trusted in a creative power that was higher than all people and the universe without the essence of the Bible or Christ's redemption. The Indian came, by divine providence, to know the same God as the Christian but in a more impending way to succumb to superstition versus learning the will of God through Christ and the Bible. Throughout the weeks that remained, Fr. Otto had the privilege to try and convey to these people that Jesus Christ is the way, the truth and the life, the very doorway to God. Too many people throughout the world have succumbed to everything and anything but the truth! But as God has tried to reveal to us the invisible through the visible in His Son; Fr. Otto tried to reveal the truth to the Blackfoot people by sharing the truth and not forcing a change for we can learn from each other.

Fr. Otto enjoyed watching the interaction between family and clans and especially enjoyed Spotted Owl and Red Wolf. The time had come for White Eagle to reveal some of the Indian ways and traditions to Spirit Heart and indeed he was ready to learn.

White Eagle drew a large circle on the ground with an arrow to signify the world. Then he drew six lines representing six families with a common root tongue. As White Eagle pronounced the names of the families, Spirit Heart tried to visualize their spelling as he scribbled the words in the back of his Bible. The Algonkian family to which belonged the Blackfoot tribe also included the Cheyenne, Arapaho, Crees and a few other tribes that Fr. Otto had difficulty in spelling. White Eagle with his arrow showed the direction and expanse of area that they lived which included just about the whole north area including parts of Canada and the northeast United States. Then there were the Athabaskan family, the Caddoan family, the Kiowan family and the Siouan family of many tribes such as the Assiniboines, Sioux, Omahas and Osages. The last family of the Great Plains was the Shoshonean family that included the tribes of the Comanches and Utes. White Eagle hit the ground many times as he said the name of Shoshones for they were dreaded enemies of the Blackfoot and causes for many battles in war.

It was accredited to the Great White Spirit that in his wisdom as the Creator and overseer of life made the buffalo for the Indian. The buffalo is held in high regard in their religion and all ways of life for all good things come from this beast. There is no way to know the actual count of the beast but it was estimated that there were some eighty million buffalo roaming this earth at the beginning of the 1800s. Being a migratory animal, hence all Indian tribes were migratory too for they lived dependent upon the buffalo. Where the buffalo roamed so too did the Indian tribes. Even though the grasslands of the plains were huge there were just too many beasts to graze and feed in one place and so as the cycle of life continued the buffalo would split into smaller roaming herds. Usually one herd would graze in the east while another graze in the west coming together and migrate north into Canada and split with one herd turning east and the other west throughout the grasslands of Alberta, Saskatchewan, and Manitoba. Depending on the bellowing of the bulls to find out which ones would be king bulls of their own herds, there could be two to four herds roaming this earth at the same time. Through the cycle of nature heading into Canada in the summer and returning to the United States in the fall, passports weren't needed. As White Eagle explained their fate upon the beasts to Spirit Heart, they walked around the campsite and Fr. Otto couldn't help but noticed smaller groups within the compound each with their own tasks. A group of young maidens making baskets, another group of elderly women making moccasins while another group of braves were making arrows with fine craftsmanship divided the chores and tasks throughout the village. There had to be some twenty groups in all for there were some at the river washing laundry, others repairing canoes and other elders giving instruction to young braves. Organized, busy and happy meant for a life of contentment and most Indians were very happy with their existence. Suicide was unheard of within the Indian tribes although if one was unhappy, for whatever reason, a squabble, lost bride or whatever, they just walked away and left the tribe. Everything in life had its place and moment for even when it came to death which is part of the end cycle of life, an elderly person just walked into the woods and died.

There was much excitement within the camp for a herd of buffalo was sighted three days from the campsite. Fr. Otto was intrigued and amazed to all the preparation, ceremony and fanfare that were given to the buffalo hunt. Tonight, there would be the buffalo dance, the calling of the buffalo ceremony, smoking of the pipe for good hunting as braves prepared to hunt and squaws prepared utensils' and baskets to retrieve all parts of the buffalo. Everyone within the Indian camp took part in the buffalo hunt from the warrior braves who would chase and ride alongside to kill the mighty beast to the squaws and children old enough to carry baskets to retrieve all useable parts of the animal.

The day of the hunt the entire tribe hides behind the hills so the buffalo are unaware to what is about to happen and remain quiet. Then the mighty yell of, "Hoka hey" which means charge as all braves surge over the hills with their bow and arrows ready to wound the beast and the warriors ready with their lances to kill the beast. The thunderous roar of galloping hooves, the racing alongside with the beasts, the shooting of arrows, the thrust of the lance along with a cloud of dust and a brown trail to be seen for miles gave Fr. Otto a snapshot into the lives of the Blackfoot Indian for everything centers around the buffalo hunt. Once the dust settles then the tedious work of retrieving all parts of the buffalo begins. Horse and dog drawn travois are led to carry the rawhides and buckskins which will be made into moccasins, winter robes, tipi covers and pouches. Then the beast is butchered and the meat carved into strips for hanging to dry out and stacked on many travois so there would be meat throughout the winter for all. Once this was done then the gathering of the hair to be made into ropes, ornaments and headdresses along with the horns, tails, skulls and even the beards weaved into ornamental decorations. Then the muscles would be skinned out used for making thread and cinches. Then the bones would be gathered to be carved and fashioned into knives, arrowheads, shovels and war clubs. They would even make game dice out of the bones which all ages enjoyed. Even the four-chambered stomach and buffalo chips were saved. Nothing went to waste. And to the victor went the spoils, the warriors that brought down the mighty beast got the delicacy of the tongue, heart and liver which they ate raw. Even when some of the gracious warriors offered some of these delicacies to Father Otto he simply replied that he was graciously full!

The Indian camp is hustling and bustling with much activity for many weeks after a buffalo hunt. Groups are organized for the multiple tasks that need to be performed. Father Otto wanted to do his part and joined Song Bird along with Red Wolf in their group. Rawhide from the buffalo, which could be bent without cracking, is used for tipi covers and for the manufacture of waterproof receptacles. Whereas the buckskin can be softened by bone scraping to be made pliable after fleshing the buffalo hides and make all sorts of clothing. Song Bird's group worked with the rawhide to be stretched and cut into the pattern for a tipi cover. The young children from adolescence to age five always join the groups along with their mothers to learn the many task of keeping a camp proficient. The older youths from age five to twelve join the elders to make accessories for the tipi and so Spotted Owl joined this group. Then the young braves from age twelve to sixteen join the fathers to learn to make weapons and train to use them in battle. Once the young braves are proficient in making and using the weapons then and only then do they become an apprentice trained for the hunt and battle to defend the camp. There are many groups to accomplish the many deeds that need to be done. Father Otto enjoyed the camaraderie and a chance to practice the Blackfoot tongue to which he was becoming very proficient. Now when he sat with White Eagle to learn about the Blackfoot's traditions, he also took the time to explain his ways and traditions in his faith. A busy camp that was doing, learning and serving was a happy camp and a community that grew in love. Father Otto reflected that this is what church is all about and in turn in the doing, learning and serving together giving worship and praise to Him above.

He was amazed at the intricate design of the tipi cover which was made in one whole piece from many buffalo hides. Cut to a pattern from memory with many loops for lashing it tight to the poles and securing it with stakes to the ground. Depending on the size of the clan, a tipi was anywhere from fifteen, twenty or greater feet in diameter with a cut out for the door opening always facing east for the rising sun which reminded them for morning worship. Most tribes were very religious and observed daily prayer ritual which Father Otto enjoyed. Within the tipi there were a place for the fireplace in the center and adjacent to the door opening. There were hide door covers for the colder, winter months but not necessary for the warmer summer months. Behind the fireplace an altar for prayer, smoking of the peace pipe and daily rituals which was strictly observed by most tribes and not just the Blackfoot. Beds on mats outlined the outer perimeter of the tipi with a place for firewood and utensils for a very utilitarian design which could be taken down in three minutes and put back up in fifteen minutes always ready for the migratory journey. Every three weeks there were mesmerizing dances and vision- seeking rites to ward off evil spirits and seek aid from the Great White Spirit to send off small war parties to reconnoiter their territory to defend against predators and enemy tribes. Chief Brave Hawk believed that a good defense was to always be on the offense.

Tonight, Father Otto was to learn about the Sun dance, and he in turn was to explain to White Eagle about the Son of God which is one of the mysteries even for a Christian. He brought along two extra bibles, one was for Running Bear and the other was for his good friend, White Eagle. As Running Bear was learning the Blackfoot tongue, Father Otto hoped Running Bear would help White Eagle with English to read the bible. He also brought three rosaries, one for each of his nephews and one for White Eagle as he tried to explain the crucifix the best he could that Christ died for each one of us. White Eagle had never heard this before but was touched by such words and closed his eyes as he grasped the crucifix and bowed his head. When Father Otto gave the rosaries to his nephews, he got down on his knees, blessed them and placed the rosaries over their heads and said to them, "Peace be with you!"

The color of the leaves was changing and frost was part of the morning dew signaling fall was approaching and Father Otto understood that time had come for him to leave and for the Indian camp to move on to new hunting grounds. His heart ached for these people, and it was good to see his Brother Kurt again along with his family. Big John Dawson walked into the camp and the boys wanted one more swim with their Un'kl O and so once again Un'kl O put on the breechclout and felt like a little kid. It was airy, comfortable without any pinch, stink or sweat as they ran to the lake for a swim. Even Big John Dawson joined in the fun as he made a big splash which delighted Spotted Owl and Red Wolf and the rest of the tribe.

That night as the stars were shining and the moon was high in the sky, Brother Kurt left the tipi and Song Bird looked over to Father Otto and placing her finger to her lips to be silent, motioned for Father Otto to follow his brother. As he stepped out from the tipi Fr. Otto watched his brother climb the winding path to the top of the mountain. Then, for the first time, he heard his brother sing a beautiful ballad that touched his heart for when he sang there was no lisp or impediment to his words.

"Tears of my Life"
The tears of my eyes blur the visions to see,
A life of many hardships as many journey across the sea.

Lives to begin anew, with fresh hopes and new dreams,
To build a home, raise a family and plant our fields
it seems.
Surreal at times, I wonder if I have everlasting
strength,
To persevere, push on and go the entire length.
The tears of my heart pull and tug at my very soul,
Through courage and prayer, we seek and take the toil.
The tears of our soul at the end we come to thee,
The Giver of all life; We thank our Blessed Trinity.

Father Otto closed his eyes, bowed his head, and listened attentively to the beautiful song. Sunrise ushered in a myriad of sounds from all the birds singing their morning songs and many emotions surged within Father Otto as he arose with White Eagle to say their last morning prayer together. It was a time for prayer, reflection, to say his goodbyes and give well wishes to a people he came to know and love. He learned so much of the people and traditions of the Blackfoot tribe and of the legend of "FT," his brother, who was frank in his words, ferocious as a bear, firm in his faith and fabulous in song. As big John Dawson led Father Otto down the mountainside, the Blackfoot people were preparing to migrate once again to a new location for sunrise brings a new day.

Chapter 8
Canada or Bust

It was a sunny cool day in spring with some remnants of snow still on the ground and you could see your breath in the air with every exhale. Family, friends and colleagues were gathered to pay their last respects to a man who some loved, respected and admired. The tombstone read, "Gustavus Bergstrom 1831 – 1893; A Son of Canada; He Served Her Well".

Even though Gustavus was born in Sweden, he accomplished so much for Canada that indeed he was considered a son along with other compatriots that did so much for Canada. As the coffin was lowered into that hollow, dark hole, sentiments surge your emotions for a last goodbye as he embarks on a new spiritual journey. Family, friends, members of parliament, union members and strangers parade by the gravesite to pay their last respects or to see if indeed that there was a coffin. Only a select few knew that the coffin in the ground was empty and that Gustavus was still alive and well, convalescing at a military compound in Saskatchewan. Major General Smet of the NWMP felt it better for concealment to protect both Gus and his family until these dastardly bastards that committed this atrocity are brought to justice. The assassination attempt which was well orchestrated and every detail planned triggered something bigger than anyone could expect.

Lucas Bergstrom was now a major partner of his law firm, and when news broke of the assassination attempt on his father's life, a moral thread snapped within him. He covertly met with a small group of highly influential people who had the wealth, means and chutzpah to undertake a necessary coup de grace for society's preservation. There is a purpose to law and order, but when the law of the land fails then and only then the right of preservation takes over. Whether it is marshal law, war or vendetta as the skilled surgeon cuts out the cancer to preserve the body, the evil must be eradicated to protect society. The church called it the crusades, when nations fail it is called war, when Texas was rampart with lawlessness, the Texas Rangers were formed and when Canada was losing to organize crime the Black Hood Annihilators were formed. A secret society of Mounties handpicked by both Major General Smet and Lucas with the consent of the Prime Minister to form a group known as the Six-packs. Each group would have six men trained in the art of covert intelligence and annihilation. From Quebec to Halifax in the east to Winnipeg and Vancouver in the west, all Canadian providences created secretive headquarters to counter crime and espionage. Wired together these groups are there to remove the quagmire before it destroys society. Through the intelligence of the networks, information was gathered about the hit sanctioned on Gustavus Bergstrom and others in political power that came from four crime families located in Chicago, New York and New Jersey. A hit list was made of the crime bosses, legal counsel and actual hit men and consigned to groups of the BHA. At the same time a list of the leaders of the Métis People that aided and abetted in the assassination attempt were given to the NWMP to apprehend.

There isn't much constraint to cross the boarders from Canada to the United States in the late 1800's and as quickly as a humming bird darts from one flower to another, the hit squads went to their designated towns by train in America and were ready to commit the unthinkable. Each team had four weeks to get into position, reconnoiter their victims and choose the right location to commit the hit. A place where there are no witnesses, limited access, and some noise abatement such as an alley, elevator, or basement.

May of 1893 saw two major events that year, first there was the Columbian Exposition and secondly on Memorial Day twelve unsuspecting derelicts from organized crime had black hoods placed over their heads each with a small symbol of a maple leaf on it; then a shotgun was placed next to their heads and the rest is history. The message sent to organized crime was loud and clear, "Stay out of Canada!"

Due to this calamity and a financial panic that led to a four-year depression within the United States, President Cleveland called the Prime Minister of Canada and eloquently asked, "What the hell is going on?"

The prime minister, prepared for such a call, responded, "Why Mr. President what do you mean?"

Still irate as a wounded tiger, he yelled, "Really, a maple leaf on all of the hoods and you don't think that our law enforcement can't put two and two together? An unsanctioned hit in my country?"

A reserved but calm Prime Minister replied, "For that I owe you a deep apology, but I didn't want to compromise the mission.

Finally, an agreeable accordance was reached, and they amicably ended their conversation.

During this period, times were rough for Canada as well as the United States for since the death of Prime Minister Macdonald; there are four successive Prime Ministers that probably wished they were somewhere else other than in charge of Canada.

Politicians have the arduous task to bring a sound economy for prosperity to their nation, peace if possible and jobs so that most people can earn a living. All the rest is fundamental but due to extreme circumstances in life, the ways and means to find solutions to those problems can be daunting. No matter what the circumstances are that we face in life our inner faith to do right is probably the one attribute that is vital. What pushes us to move forward, encounter insurmountable odds, to be a hero and have the integrity to stand up for others? All of us are given a soul, a conscience, a heart, and a free will, but none of these are worth anything without the gift of faith! Life's many complex and daunting problems are never-ending and cause many to falter in life to make the wrong choices. Lucas reached a turning point in his life where he crossed the line and needed help to find his way back.

Gustavus struggled daily in his workout to make progress so that one day he could walk through the hospital doors and go home. Unbeknown of the sanctioned hit devised by his son, he wasn't prepared for the uncertainty of his son's consequences. It was a pleasant surprise when Wilhelm made an unannounced visit to see his old friend and boss. Major General Smet wanted every precaution taken with no communication to alert anyone about the status of Gustavus. Top priority was given for keeping Gus alive.

Gus exclaimed as he viewed Wilhelm walk into his room with Major General Smet, "Well, what a great sight for these old eyes," as Gus got up to embrace Wilhelm.

Then he shook Major General Smet's hand and was elated to have some company as he said, "It's a long train ride to just see a friend."

The major general started the conversation with, "I'm afraid it's both business and pleasure."

Gus, giving a smile, said, "Great, I'm ready for both for I've had enough of convalescing!"

The major general brought Gus up to speed with the creation of the BHA and their first assignment which was a total success. Gus was both impressed and pleased and asked, "Whose brain child conceived this brilliant idea?"

His expression turned dire when the major general broke the news that it was his son.

With a somber voice, he said, "A toxic organization for a perilous world!"

Then Wilhelm broke into the conversation by showing a bottle of Jack Daniels that he smuggled into the room.

"Oh, marvelous, I've been ready for that for a very long time," as he got three glasses.

Gus raised his glass and said, "To friendships!"

Then the major general brought them both up to speed with the blessings of the prime minister about the development of the BHA and the covert groups known as the six-packs. Gus got a kick from the covert group's name.

With another round of drinks, Gus was ready to settle down, roll up his sleeves and tackle some business.

Throughout the next decade life wasn't easy for Gus with the passing of his wife, Elsa, an assassination attempt on his son, the grueling demands of the BHA on his son with the intelligence service and his failing health; everything became a struggle. The trip to Maine to see his grandson, Adam, get married made him wonder if he had let life slip through his fingers as he reflected over the pass twenty-eight years. The coming to America in 1874 seemed like yesterday but now it is 1903 and as the passage in the bible claims that wisdom preserves the life of its owner, Gus wondered if he had any wisdom at all.

While sitting at his desk at the parliament building, Gus admired the picture of his grandson's wedding. Adam and his new bride made a stunning couple, as most couples do, as he started his career at the shipyard. Just then Wilhelm walked into his office and placed a thick file on Gus desk.

"Here is Project 2436 on natural resources for Panama development," he said as Wilhelm sat down across from him.

The file was two inches thick with requisitions, maps, and blueprints for the development of the Panama Ditch better known as the Panama Canal. The briefing took three hours to bring Gus up to speed as he whistled at the magnitude of the project. Construction was to begin in the summer of 1904 and was projected to be completed in ten years with an estimated cost at $380,000,000.00.

Gus sat back in his chair and just shook his head as he said, "Can you imagine what this means for the countries that get involved in the project of this magnitude? Why, the economy will rebound three-fold, and jobs will surge to the breaking point!"

Wilhelm handed a list of natural resources that Canada could furnish if we could get our foot in the door with the United States as a primary supplier. The United States Army Corp of Engineers oversaw the construction project.

Gus snapped his fingers as he made a list of names to be delegates to Washington DC to meet with the Secretary of the Interior and President Theodore Roosevelt. Time was not to be wasted as Gus said, "Wilhelm, opportunity very seldom knocks on your door with such a gift, the gift to get both Canada and the United States into an economic boom. Now is the time for definitive action and Canada has the lumber and other natural resources that can fill the bill."

Gus' mind was racing as Wilhelm asked the question, "What else do we need to prepare for this trip?"

"Well," Gus replied as he reached for his pipe, "we will need at least three more logging camps on our west coast with all lumber brought to Vancouver and shipped from there to Panama."

"Then extend the railways northward for a supply line between the logging camps and Vancouver!"

"But enough of that; let's get cracking and organize this delegation and book our trip to Washington before the United States decides that they have enough lumber to fill the job. The only other competitor big enough and close enough is Brazil. But screw them all to hell; this is money in our pockets!"

This news reenergized Gus and he was ready to get back to work and stop his galley-lagging around.

The meeting at the White House was anything but cordial, the 26th President of the United States, Theodore Roosevelt, was prepared with a dossier on each delegate from the prime minister on down the chain of command which included a condemnation from the previous President, Grover Cleveland. The condemnation was for the President's eyes only as it read, "Shoot the bastards!"

But the Prime Minister and Gus also had dossiers on the president and his staff. Gus was very interested in meeting President Theodore Roosevelt for this man didn't only have integrity and courage but the necessary chutzpah to get things done! He was a former New York City's Police Commissioner, the organizer of the Rough Riders that charged up San Juan's hill, and as interim president due to the assassination of President McKinley, dissolved the Northern Securities Co. for violating antitrust laws. As far as Gus was concerned, this man is a straight shooter.

The prime minister was introduced to the president and after a few cordial banters; Gustavus Bergstrom was introduced to the president.

"Indeed, no introduction is necessary; this is the man that was shot in an assassination attempt and has made Canada economically sound," President Roosevelt firmly gripped Gus's hand and continued, "I am very pleased that you could make this meeting!"

Gustavus replied, "Well, Mr. President I was concerned about our reception for the next person you're about to meet is my son, Lucas who founded the BHA."

The president turns to eye Lucas and responds, "So it was your dad whom you were trying to protect?"

Lucas replied, "Yes, Sir, and I am afraid I owe this country and your office an apology!"

The president very sternly considered the countenance of Sebastian before asking, "Tell me son, if you had to do it over what would you change?"

Lucas never blinked or hesitated but replied, "With all due respect Sir, not a damn thing!"

The president roared with laughter and said, "Splendid, I like this guy, please call me Teddy!"

The ice was broken, and the rest of the meeting went extremely well with Canada getting the contract to furnish the necessary lumber and other natural resources for the Panama Canal project. There was one added benefit for both sides as Lucas and the president became good friends as the president commented, "This young man reminds me of myself when I was young and full of piss and vinegar!"

"But now," the president continued, "I'm just full of vinegar."

Later that afternoon the president asked for Lucas and Major General Smet to sit with some of his advisors and tell them about the BHA. From that meeting, the president felt that the United States needed such an organization and in the following years the birth of the Federal Bureau of Investigation was born, better known as the FBI for internal law enforcement. Many years later due to foreign espionage, a separate branch for national security known as the CIA was formed.

The rain, which had been falling steadily for four days, had turned the trail into a sloppy river of mud. At times, it was a torrential downpour causing no visibility beyond your hands reach. This wouldn't be the worst of Mother Nature for at higher elevations this precipitation will be snow. Traveling through the mountains and forest of British Columbia was slow and cumbersome but time is of the essence to push on and survey the land. Train tracks must be laid, tunnels blasted through mountain sides and bridges to traverse river gorges needed to be built to carry the precious cargo of lumber to Vancouver. Deadlines had to be met and if Canada wanted to be a major supplier for the Panama Canal Project; no excuses were acceptable. The outfit of Dutchman Northwest Survey & Engineering Co. Inc. was contracted to survey the land to push three lines for the logging camps. They were the largest outfit with 125 surveying units and a reputation to get the job done. With 366,000 square miles, British Columbia is considered the jewel of North America like an oasis in the desert, Canada's only Pacific Coast province. Large tracts of timber laden slopes covering three fourths of the province rich in game, fish and minerals will bring an untold wealth to Canada if only it can be gotten, hence the vital importance to get the rail lines laid and the valuable product transported.

The first of three surveying teams would push up the Fraser River from the south along with the second team venturing by the Skeena River from the west and the last team heading north from Prince George up the Finley River and turning east. A forest so vast had to be attacked from three sides with three logging camps to be cleared and installed overnight. Clearing the land and harvesting the timber required manpower beyond comprehension. To remain competitive to harness the resources and manpower to be cost effective, a new way of thinking was needed. A paradigm shift was about to take place as Gus engineered a new plan for the railroads. Portable saw mills on trains to move from logging camp to logging camp would save time, money and manpower. If this could be accomplished, then schedules and deadlines could be met. But this wasn't the only problem looming over the horizon.

Just when you think the gears are turning well, a spanner wrench is thrown into the cog wheel of life to cause everything to come to a screeching halt. Once again Gus had to call on the law firm of Audet, Farnsworth, & La-Pointe and with Lucas now a major partner, the name has changed to AFL & Bergstrom. Overseeing the BHA and a major law firm kept Lucas busy as ever. Territorial dispute between the United States and the United Kingdom, which controlled Canada's foreign relations, erupted over the Alaska and Canadian boundary. The territorial dispute had been going back and forth like a tennis ball first in one court and then in another between the Russian and British Empires and then when the United States purchased Alaska in 1867 the volley continued between the British and United States causing much indigestion and pain. Boundaries aren't necessary for a territory where a few Indians live and there are no cities or towns, hence no need for local government or law enforcement until a spark is lit that causes a population explosion. That spark was the Klondike gold rush! More than 30,000 men, women, and even children persevered through the Chilkoot Trail and climbed the daunting Golden Stairs during the Klondike gold rush in the Yukon. During that period, some 100,000 fortune seekers moved through Alaska to the Klondike gold region. The presence of gold and a large population greatly increased the importance of the area and the desirability of fixing an exact boundary. Then towns like Dawson and others sprang up with land claims, claim jumpers, criminals and the need for government and law enforcement. Lawlessness became so rampart that a few guns weren't enough to stop the violence and so the NWMP brought in Gatling guns to defend the territory which caused uproar from Dawson to Skagway loud enough that it could be heard all the way to the capitals of Ottawa and Washington DC. Boundaries, government and law enforcement needs became the cry of the land.

Canada had more to lose than acreage of land on one side of a border; its future growth, wealth and economy was contingent on the contract deal for the Panama Canal. Gus cautioned his son that an amicable way to resolve this predicament is through arbitration versus war. Finally, with much finesse the Hay-Herbert Treaty between the United States and Britain entrusted the decision to arbitration by a mixed tribunal of six members: three Americans, two Canadians, and one Briton.

Gus smiled as he lit his pipe, sat back in his big chair and allowed the tribunal to do its job. Then he said to his son, "Compromise is an art for both politicians and lawyers to achieve your end!" Lucas learned an invaluable lesson from his dad about a laissez-faire attitude of letting things take their own course and if all else fails then go through arbitration and leave war as a last resort.

A boom time erupted throughout Northwest America between gold strikes, multiple jobs and golden opportunism for investments. Boom towns, sea ports, rail lines, and shops sprung up all along the Pacific Northwest and as the population grew so did the demand for food and supplies. An infrastructure of roads besides rail is needed to improve the transportation mode for moving people and goods.

Parliament is in session, and Gustavus Bergstrom is presenting Project 2436, which is Appropriation Funds for Resources Development. The disappointment and anger in Canada over the Alaska boundary dispute is still seething, and Gus needed to find a way to appease most of his colleagues to obtain a quorum of votes. He presented a seven-step developmental plan for the next decade for:

- Forestry Development/Lumber for Panama Canal Project
- Rail Development for Northwest Canada
- Energy Development on Great Lakes
- Shipping Development/West Coast & Great Lakes
- Manufacturing Development
- Mineral Development & Fur Trade
- Sea Ports & Fisheries Development

The seven-step plan would bring manufacturing jobs to all provinces, energy resources to power industry and a boom in the economy. Project 2436 and his seven-step plan passed overwhelmingly, and Gus once again had his desk piled sky high with projects. Some projects were involved, costly and complicated such as rail development in the Cordilleran Region of British Columbia due to tunnels blasted through the mountains and bridges to be built which required enormous manpower and supplies and you never knew which one would dry up first. Everybody wanted a job but some quickly got tired of the long hours, loneliness and backbreaking pain. With the thousands of man-hours came multiple deaths from the elements and fatal accidents from landslides, falling trees and wildlife.

The fur trappers were called in to clear out the wild grizzly bears, mountain lions, moose and mountain goats to protect the workers, put meat on their tables with fresh game and to collect the purses for furs. Besides the big game there were marten, weasels, wolverines, badgers and river otters that brought a commanding price for the pelts. It also brought some familiar faces to the region as Big John Dawson and his family migrated to the region to try their luck and fortune on the new bounty of furs. Big John was now married to an Indian squaw from the Blackfoot Tribe known as Spring Flower and they had five sons all of age to shoot a rifle and trap for fur. With game in Montana vanishing and the buffalo herds migrating, Big John wanted to try his fortune in Canada. Walking into the trading post at Moose Jaw Pass on the Fraser River just north of Williams Lake to get some supplies, he meets Andrew Duncan first surveyor of the first surveying team heading north.

Due to Big John's colossal size Andrew introduced himself by saying, "Hey, big fella, what's yur name?"

After some introductions and firm hand shakes, "I want yu to meet another big fella; I'd say about the same size, not sur though, hey Big Bob cum here and meet Big John!"

They could have been book ends with Big John a might bigger and a bit taller by a hair. But Big Bob with his quick wit said, "I'm the handsome one with a devil's gleam in both eyes for the pretty lasses!"

Andrew asked Big John what he was doing in these parts and he explained how he and his family came from the Fort Benton, Montana area. That his wife is from the Blackfoot Tribe in northern Montana and as the tribe migrated into Alberta, Canada to follow the buffalo, they decided to turn left and head for British Columbia for fur trading.

"I understand that the Hudson Bay Company is paying top dollar for all types of furs in these parts?" Big John asked.

"Yep, top dollar, the Molson bank out of Ontario has a branch up in Prince George and will give you a banker's note for all and any furs trapped or shot that is good anywhere including your United States."

"Well," Big John exclaimed, "that sounds good to me!"

"Then let me introduce you to the rest of the crew for you met Big Hatchet Bob whose nickname is Jumper."

"Why Jumper may I ask?" Big John wondered.

Andrew laughed as he explained that he jumped over all the ravines and gullies to hold the rod so they can shoot our elevations with the transits.

Then he continued to introduce Big John to Ted Tomlinson, their engineer; Tom Bismarck, their cook better known as "Spice Rack;" and Logobola better known as Raven Feather their guide. Logobola was from the Tsimshian Indian Tribe of the Northwest, one of the first indigenous tribes to settle there that goes back to the 1400s.

Andrew pressed Big John and his family to join their group for another rifle is always good protection and that there is plenty of game where they are going.

"Fine," Big John said, "we'll set up camp just across the river."

Upon agreement of the union, they decided to meet at sunrise at the trading post as the Survey crew headed towards Bear Claw Saloon for some last-minute drinks and camaraderie with the lasses.

Walking through the swinging doors to the huge saloon, Big Bob ordered a round of drinks for everyone as Logobola walked back to join the family of Big John Dawson for Indians weren't welcomed in the saloon.

Big John welcomed Logobola and introduced him to his family as they set up camp and built a camp fire. The five boys quickly gathered firewood and as they returned to the campsite Big John introduced each one to Logobola.

"This is Long Tail, who is age twelve, and here is Running Cougar, age ten, along with Howling Coyote, who is age nine. Trailing behind them is Falcon, age eight, and Bobcat, age six."

Logobola enjoyed meeting the boys as he told them that in his tribe he was known as, "Raven and in the Tsimshian language known as Yaahl."

When Spring Flower prepared supper, the boys played a number game that intrigued Logobola as he watched and listened.

"Ni't, Naatsi, Niookska, Niiso', Niisito," which meant one to five in Blackfoot words. Logobola quickly got on his knees and repeated the numbers in Blackfoot words which amused the boys because of his accent and then said them again in Tsimshian words as, "K'uul, Gu'pl, K'wili, Txaalpx, Kwstuns," as the boys enjoyed hearing the numbers in his language. Then Logobola pointed to the boys to try the numbers in the Tsimshian language. All the boys enjoyed this game of going back and forth in their native tongue as Logobola pointed to the rising moon and said, "Gyemgmaatk." Each of the boys tried to master the word and then pointed to the moon and said in their native tongue, "Ko'komiki'somma." Already strong bonds of friendship were beginning to form as Spring Flower watched from a distance and enjoyed the word games.

The tempo of noise that echoed from the Bear Claw Saloon got a bit rowdy as the evening grew long and the ladies of the evening came out to play. Big Bob jumped up and wanted to dance with the first pretty lady he saw and did the jig to everyone's delight for he was limber and quick on his feet considering his large frame size as he danced the evening away. Then he grabbed for another young lovely and ushered the two girls through the crowd as he said, "Ah, my darlings, let us proceed up these stairs where I will make your eyebrows rise, put a smile on your lips, cause your pubic hairs to dance and curl your toes to the merriment of Big Bob."

Just then a drunken Spice Rack, who was inspired by Big Bob's antics, jumped up to follow pursuit of another beauty. Now no one knew the age of Spice Rack because he had possession of two birth certificates. But judging from the birth years on either one, he was either 75 or 76 years old and still kicking as he said to this one young beauty while grabbing a bottle of brandy, 'Come on my darling, I will put a frown on your face, step on your toes causing your bunions to hurt and if my King George doesn't rise to the occasion, then we will enjoy this bottle of brandy for the rest of the evening!'" That brought a round of cheers and laughter from everyone in the establishment.

Logobola arose before sunrise to build a fire and gather some wood as Big John and Spring Flower got up and made breakfast for the boys. Sunrise brings a new day and as the sun peeked over the horizon, Logobola pointed to the sun and said, "Gimgmdziws."

Each of the boys pointed in turn to the sun and repeated the word for sun and then said in Blackfoot, "Ki'somma."

Logobola in turn pointed to the sun and repeated the word and so a new day of word games begin with smiles and friendships. All of them were accounted for by full sunrise including hangovers from some to meet at the trading post and start their journey. Hangovers in those days were never used as an excuse to not pull your own weight as the pack mules were loaded and ready.

Over the next few months elevations were shot, a trail was blazed and Big John and his family bagged many furs making it a very profitable season. Throughout the trip between Spice Rack with his assortment of spices and Spring Flower with her many recipes, the food was scrumptious, tasty and just plain good.

The night before heading back to Moose Jaw Pass, Spice Rack got up and walked into the bushes to relieve himself when he walked across the path of an unsuspecting grizzly bear. I'm not sure who was more startled but the angry bear reared on his hind legs and took a swipe with those huge claws and gashed poor old Spice Rack across his entire chest ripping open a gigantic wound. An ungodly yell echoed out as it awoke everyone in the camp. Big John was the first to spring to his feet, draw his 30" Arkansas Bowie knife with a 24" blade, three inches wide and jumped on to the back of that old grizzly. He then plunged that Bowie into the back neck of the bear multiple times until the bear collapsed. Old Spice Rack never made sunrise but died gasping his last breath with his last words of, "Bless me Father."

There are many things that one can teach to another about life, God, survival, friendship and the list goes on but one thing that is extremely difficult to teach about are the feelings of death as Big John tried to comfort and console his boys. They all took a genuine liking to Spice Rack, his stories, his candy fingers that he made for the boys and his fatherly friendship. He took the time to play, teach and pass a bit of himself to each of the boys. That final goodbye is never easy as Big Bob and Logobola dug a gravesite and Andrew took off a board from one of the crates to make a tombstone. With his knife, he carved,

Tom Bismarck
"Spice Rack"
A True Friend
RIP

The body was neatly wrapped in a blanket, lowered into the gravesite, and Logobola laid two claws from the bear that he had cut off as Ted gave the final eulogy.

"Here lies Spice Rack, our friend, who enjoyed life immensely and it is only through the door of death that we can enter the hereafter and it teaches us to appreciate the gift of life a little better and to take the time to say, *Thank You God for this time on Earth.* Amen."

Logobola stood between the boys and then got down on his knees to give each young brave a bear claw as a memento. He hugged each one and told them to be brave, as Spice Rack was a brave man. With a final prayer and a look at the gravesite they departed and headed south towards Moose Jaw Pass. Death and goodbyes are never easy in this life, but for those who are humble enough to believe in the hereafter, it teaches us to be appreciative for our Lord and Savior. Amen

As the seasons passed, the surveyors finished their job and the extensive construction began as crews built rail lines, bridges and tunnels. Three logging camps were added to the region; timber was cut, sawed and transported to the seaports of Vancouver and again labor issues erupted. The railroad came through with flatbeds converted to a makeshift sawmill as the logs were made into proper timber length and width. Progress never stands still and as quickly as the old aggravated problems are solved, new ones are created. As science and technology advances and rapid industrialization expands, the plight of the migratory clan vanishes and the transformation of towns and cities abound. Industry supersedes agriculture as the main source of livelihood. With the influx of people came the need and demand for better transportation, communications, provisions and dwellings. Factories along with fisheries, canneries and more industry replaced the trading post and police departments began replacing the existing forts for protection.

The wheels of Parliament were turning out more laws and land reform for large scale industrial exploitation of mineral resources than Canadian geese migrating south for the winter. Canada has a vast land and with it a vast richness in mineral resources that are used in all other industries. The metals obtained from ores are used in machinery and electrical equipment, as well as in bridges and buildings. Mineral salt is used in foods and industrial processes. The metals are even needed to coin our very mint. The list of uses goes on and on as well as the regulation to govern all our natural resources. Parliament was busy indeed trying to keep up with all the demands for minerals, fuels and protecting the land. British Columbia was rich in both forests for logging and minerals for mining but mines in the Canadian Shield produced not only precious metals but, increasingly critical base metals such as copper, lead, silver and zinc. The Canadian Shield covers some 1,850,000 square miles. That is half the size of the country and is shaped like a horseshoe with Hudson Bay in the open part of the horseshoe. Gus kept the law firms busy with new regulations for mining, labor laws to appease worker rights and protection and a new growing concern over the ecology that we are raping the environment. And to the amazement of Gus his favorite drink of Jack Daniels wasn't enough to keep up with the rigors of the time. A new concocted round of drinks, one Drambuie, two Glenlivet Scotches, three Jack Daniels and a shot of Tequila was what the doctor ordered. Some damn guy in the merchant marine who was also in the monastery came up with the concoction. It works! Tomorrow is a new day, for tonight I will fade into oblivion with my new-found concoction and leave chance to tomorrow. Gus was proud of the accomplishments during his tenure for the land that was settled on in British Columbia and the northwest was considered inaccessible until I pushed the rail lines and roads. Now there are many jobs due to logging, mining and industry; towns and cities are burgeoning and opportunities abounding.

The seventh prime minister of Canada is Sir Wilfrid Laurier the first French-Canadian to rise to the power from being a lawyer, journalist and now politician. He and Gus became consummate friends and a comrade for ideals to "Build up Canada" is their common goal and watchword for Parliament. Being raised Roman Catholic, he was partial to creating jobs for the middle class and a better way of life. It was Laurier's liberal immigration policy that brought hundreds of thousands of settlers to the western provinces. As quickly as Gus conceived plans to further develop Canada, Parliament and the prime minister overwhelmingly approved many of them. From the logging camps to the sea ports for shipment of lumber for the Panama Canal project, to mining exploitation and industrial expansion and now energy development through hydropower with dams throughout the great lakes; Canada made gigantic strides towards economic development and prosperity.

President Teddy Roosevelt indeed wanted to christen the new deal for the Panama Canal project and invited Prime Minister Laurier, Gus and his son Lucas to his hunting lodge in South Dakota's Black Hills National Forest for a mixture of business and pleasure. At the meeting was also the secretary of interior for the United States, Ethan A. Hitchcock along with other distinguished guests. The

Panama Deal was not the only priority on the agenda but a joint effort between Canada and the United States was presented for the great lakes development of shipping lanes through a series of canals and joint energy development through a series of dams to be built. It was a meeting that dreams are built on and bright futures are blossomed. The four-day meeting began each morning with a robust breakfast of fresh game, juice, coffee and eggs all exquisitely fixed to your fancy followed by a round of sharp shooting at the target range. Then the agenda continued by meetings and more meetings with lunch, horseback riding and cocktails. A delightful barbecue at night followed by fly-fishing for those that enjoyed the sport and another round of cocktails. Such camaraderie is essential in the political arena if deals are to be forged between countries and if permanent agreements are to be made. The pen is mightier than the sword to cement deals and the drink along with a handshake to make friendly bonds.

There was a crusty looking individual that was at the lodge but not present at the meetings who was finally introduced to all as sculptor Gutzon Borgium. On their third night at the meeting, he revealed a plan that he had been working on for a couple of years; the gigantic carved sculptures depicting the faces of four U. S. Presidents on the southeastern face of Mount Rushmore. Presidents George Washington, Thomas Jefferson, Abraham Lincoln and Theodore Roosevelt would be immortalized in stone. A thunderous roar of applause could be heard when Teddy Roosevelt's name was mentioned which brought a boyish, broad smile to his face. Funds still had to be raised and approval met by congress but in the following years the project that was to become known as the "Shrine of Democracy," would begin.

The train ride back to Ottawa was quiet and enjoyable especially when the Prime Minister asked Gus, "What do you think Gus, should Canada immortalize us in stone on some mountain top in Canada?"

Placing his pipe in the ashtray Gus replied, "My God, I'm stone enough as it is, I don't need to be immortalized in stone!"

Chapter 9
Shotgun Sheriff

Life, not death, is triumphant!

John Milton wrote that poignant phrase, and how many of us truly grasp the meaning of that phrase? Next to William Shakespeare, John Milton is regarded as the greatest English poet that ever lived. His *Paradise Lost* is considered the finest epic poem in literature.

Father Otto is back in his parish and is struggling with preparing his homily for Sunday's Mass until he reads that phrase coined by John Milton. He wants to include it into his homily because it drives the main point of our religious life into perspective. He struggles to phrase the opening sentence and so pushes himself back from the desk and kneels to pray for guidance from above. And then the words begin to flow as he continues to write his homily,

"God so loved the world that he sent his only son to make visible what has been invisible to heal, teach and show us the way of His truth. But and it is a very big but, to die for us as the unblemished lamb and to conquer death. By conquering death those who believe in Him shall have everlasting life. Yes, indeed, life, not death is triumphant thanks to our Lord and Savior, Jesus Christ! But in this life, we have choices to make before we go through the door of death, for death is only a door which can lead us to either heaven or hell!"

Father Otto continued working on his homily as the Bishop walked in and interrupted him by saying, "Glory be to God for your safe return."

Fr. Otto arose from his desk and replied, "Deo Gratias, and it is good to see you, your Excellency!"

Archbishop Napoleon Joseph Perche couldn't help but notice the artifacts in Fr. Otto's office as he pointed to the breechclout and asked, "What is that may I ask?"

Fr. Otto smiled and replied, "Freedom, freedom without the pinch!"

Fr. Otto continued smiling as he remembered how free and wonderful it felt swimming with his nephews.

Then the Archbishop pointed to the peace pipe that rested on the corner of Fr. Otto's desk and asked, "And what is the significance of that?"

Smiling and gesturing to the Archbishop to have a seat he said, "I'll make us some tea for we have much to discuss."

As Fr. Otto made the tea, the Archbishop looked around the small office and noticed many Indian artifacts especially the "Dreamcatcher" hung by the window. When Fr. Otto returned with the tea, he opened and revealed this fantastic journey to find his brother and unraveled a story of love, betrayal, fortitude and above all about a spirit. Half way through his story Fr. Otto asked the Archbishop if he ever experienced a vision and then continued with his story about the vision quest. As his own Iliad journey unfolded, Fr. Otto pointed to the many artifacts and explained their meaning and purpose. As he explained the breechclout, the Archbishop roared with laughter but when he pointed to the peace pipe and reiterated the vision, it moved the Archbishop to tears. Then pointing to the "Dreamcatcher," Fr. Otto explained the legend of how good dreams pass through the center hole to the sleeping person, while the bad dreams are trapped in the web and perish in the light of dawn. Then Fr. Otto gave one of those deep, piercing looks towards the Archbishop and asked, "How can a people who never heard of Jesus Christ have such a deep, loving spirituality?"

The Archbishop, nodding his head, replied, "God certainly does work in a mysterious and marvelous way!"

The Archbishop sincerely felt that Fr. Otto indeed had a special calling to his profession but wasn't sure at the time where the calling would lead him.

The long-awaited reunion between three brothers finally arrives and Otto is elated to see both Stefan and Wolfgang. It has been ten months since they have seen each other and the long-awaited news about their brother Kurt is indeed welcome news that he is alive and well. Over an enjoyable supper and a few drinks the conversation just flowed continuously without interruption as the night dwindled away. They learned of Song Bird and about their nephews, Spotted Owl and Red Wolf, and were greatly amused when Otto told them about their brother's new name of Running Bear. With one more order of drinks, the camaraderie rounded out the evening.

The SS *Freiheiten Suchen* brought more immigrants to New Orleans with new hopes and dreams and mail from the homeland. Within a few days, Otto received word from his brother Axel that Papa had passed away, and now both parents were deceased. Upon reading the letter, Otto bowed his head, said a short prayer, and looked up towards heaven with tears of gladness. Papa and Mama were together now in their new spiritual life and Otto would need to break the news to both of his brothers.

The parish that Fr. Otto presided over was packed to a full church with new immigrants from the old country. Throughout history many groups of people have been forced to momentous choices to stay and give up deeply, felt beliefs and convictions or leave. Many have chosen to leave rather than disavow their ideals. Fr. Otto was touched and indeed felt for the downtrodden, for once he and his brothers felt the same way. And as he began his homily, he reflected and chose his words carefully.

"My dear friends in Christ, I remember when I returned home from Rome and was forced to leave my homeland, my family and aging parents and I felt very disillusioned, afraid and weary. Come to me all of you who feel burdened and I will give you rest, says the Lord. Yes, for me and my three brothers some thirty years ago, it was extremely difficult to come to America but each of us has been comforted for it takes strength to survive but it takes courage to live in our faith."

Father Otto finished the rest of the sermon with his prepared text that he worked on with a heavy heart.

The next morning the New Orleans Gazette read, "Tom Horn is executed for the murder of a fourteen-year old boy in Cheyenne, Wyoming, on November 20, 1903.

Even in the early nineteen hundreds, there were still bank robbers, train desperadoes, murderers, thieves, rustlers, and any other low down scoundrel that ever walked on two legs could still make a slippery get-away with a fast horse throughout the west. Rangers, U.S. Marshals, and bounty hunters were busy as ever trying to round up the culprits and collect the reward that is if you could stay alive.

Why even before Ma Barker, there was Ma Butcher and her four sons Melvin, Hickory, Huey and Dick. They each carried a Winchester, Colt 45 and a meat cleaver and were the deadliest outlaws out west. They robbed anything and everything in their path from depots, banks, railroad, saloons and any individual that looked like he was worth more than two dollars. Their familiar cry of, "Reach for the sky," terrorized the west as they slashed off arms so they couldn't draw their guns and then slashed off their head, for dead people don't talk. This outrage in the early nineteen hundred caused Governor Murphy to present a Ranger Bill to the territorial legislature of Arizona which it quickly enacted. A local cattleman by the name of Burt Mossman served as its founding captain. The cry out west was "Exterminate the Vermin," and that is just what they did. The rangers chased the Butcher gang all over Arizona and finally had them caught between a rock and a hard place. Well actually between them and the canyon, The Grand Canyon! The final push was the end to Ma Butcher and her four sons as they were driven back and off the Grand Canyon. They didn't even take the time to admire the view on the way down.

President Theodore Roosevelt who has always been an avid outdoorsman and staunch conservationist had visited the Grand Canyon earlier that year and decided to wait another three years before establishing the Grand Canyon Game Preserve. Hopefully by then there would be no remains. That incident was kept out of sight, out of mind and out of the paper!

About that same time, a warrant was issued for the apprehension of the Black Hats, a notorious gang that pillaged throughout the southwest and known for wearing their black Stetsons. The leader was a desperado by the name of Joel with a bunch of the most unscrupulous band of men that the devil could muster together. First there was rancorous Rasmusson with a patch over his left eye from a knife fight. He would just as soon shoot or stab ya then talk to ya. Then there was Claude Dieffenback and smiling Sandy both from the Canadian Rockies who hunted bear and any she devils on two legs. Wrangler Rangel who came up from Mexico to take a break from the hot tamales and big Mike McKay who could press a six-hundred-pound bull over his head attached themselves to the gang like burdocks to britches. This bunch made Vickery's Vaqueros look like boy scouts.

U.S. Marshall Steve Zimmer was on their trail with the distinct orders to bring this gang in dead or alive. There was a string of robberies from Texas through Arkansas and yonder into Kansas. They were to meet their demise when the gang came into Coffeyville, Kansas for the town had an old hombre known as the "Shotgun Sheriff." He never learned to count beyond three and always told his opponents to stand ready and shoot it out for he would count to three but then shoot the scoundrels at the count of two. He carried two shotguns, two colt forty-fives and a mean disposition as he shot most bastards dead. There were very few hangings in Coffeyville. Well, long after sunset the Black Hats ride into town and saunter up to the saloon to wet their whistles. Shotgun had a couple of his deputies posted in town to keep a lookout for the bunch and to let him know when they ride into town. It was quarter to nine when the Black Hats rode into town. It was ten to nine when Shotgun walked into the saloon with his two deputies and yelled, "I'll count to three and then draw!"

Each of the Black Hats turned and faced the sheriff and his deputies.

Shotgun started to count, "One!"

And before he ever got to two, all the Black Hats drew their guns and shot the lawman dead.

It was nine o'clock when the Black Hats robbed the Wells Fargo bank and rode out of Coffeyville!

They left a trail of bank robberies and shootings throughout Kansas from Wichita to Abilene and from Abilene to Dodge. Then they headed south to Tulsa and on to Texarkana and then proceeded to Barton Rouge and New Orleans. A mighty cantankerous Marshall Zimmer followed the hard-driven trail for four months and wound up in his own backyard always a day or two behind the Black Hats. From the long dusty trail the gang was once again ready to wet their whistles as they rode up to Trahan's Alligator Saloon. A round of drinks were ordered throughout the night as the gang got a bit boisterous and started to shoot up the place. The proprietor known as a Mr. Brad Bubba Sir could contend with the noise but not the shooting and so proceeded behind the bar where there was a row of levers. Now each lever controlled a trap door under each chair within the establishment. Upon any disturbance, the proprietor just pulled the lever and the culprit fell to the gruesome death of biting, gnashing jaws of hungry alligators below. Well, when the shooting started, a Mr. Brad Bubba Sir started to pull the levers and that was the last ever heard of the Black Hats. Although there is a legend that the leader of the Black Hats, known as Joel, was too ornery to die and to this day on a clear night one can hear a "ya-hoo" as some bald dude rides that old alligator through the swamps of the bayou waving his black hat. A song has been written to the legend of the Black Hat dude.

"Life's twist & turns are never easy and sometimes it makes me feel a bit queasy,
But if yu think life is tough, try riding the back of a bronco alligator.
From sunrise to sunset in the bayou the jaws of death are there to tease me,
But if yu think life is tough, try riding the back of a bronco alligator.
First this way and slash that way, we very seldom walk a straight line,
We should not cheat, lie, steal, or do any terrible crime.
But if you think life is tough, try riding the back of a bronco alligator.
Strive to do better in life and try to help your neighbor,

With courage and faith try to walk straight and
keep the pace,
Or yu could be cut down by a sharp, reeling
saber.
Now is the time to choose, be wise and pray
with some grace,
Or yu could wind up riding the back of a
bronco alligator."

Wolfgang felt melancholy from receiving the news about
his dad from Otto and tried to remember the smiling faces
of his parents. One never forgets but time has a way to
fade clear images from our memory. He missed the laughter, cheers, and the merriment of family times; the sitting
together and saying grace at a table of plenty. The games,
the running in the snow, and experiencing life with his
brothers and sisters eased the burden of growing and learning when you have someone to share life's events with.
But this somber attitude would soon disappear as he prepared to ask the one vital question to a wife to be. For he
met a Miss Mila Bauer that made his heart soar and his
mind to day-dream, for she too was from the old country
and had eyes fixed on him. Her parents ran a bakery shop
in Memphis known as the "Rivers Flow Café and Bakery
Shop" on Beale Avenue before it became known as a street
famous for its blues music and delectable restaurants. The
shop was located across the street from Schwab's well

known for everything from their apparel to novelties and from novelties to voodoo portions. Their motto read, "If you can't find it at Schwab's, you're better off without it." Time makes it evident when to ask the question and he wanted to take Mila to New Orleans to meet his brother and ask him to marry them. Plans were set to settle in Memphis, a place rich in history, culture and the notable blues. The founders of the city laid out a plan featuring a regular grid of streets interrupted by four town squares to allow people to stop and enjoy life. The developing history wasn't always easy or in a glow as the 1870s saw more than one epidemic of yellow fever causing many deaths, tears and the departure of thousands of fleeing families. Now years later the signs of a revival in growth during the beginning 1900s, people enjoying the rich musical heritage and the culinary legacy are booming again. And who can resist the lip smacking taste of the Memphis barbecue? It felt right; Wolfgang felt at home once again for in addition to the waves of Irish, Jewish and Italian immigrants there were many Germans settling in Memphis. The date was set by the loving couple, and it was a month away before the nuptials would be proclaimed.

What a jumble mess we humans can cause, for what God has created in peace and tranquility, we humans burst asunder. Whether it is a people, a nation, or a simple two in marriage, we humans indeed burst them asunder. Sometimes it seems that God must have tears in His eyes as he sees humans desecrate and demoralize what He has created! It never ceases to amaze me the utter buffoonery of the human twit! How low is low? Every time we lower the bar, we are lowered to mediocrity and once anyone accepts that, we do not aspire to do better or improve life or even can be inspired to do better!

First, we pushed the Native Americans west, then further west and when there was no place to go, confinement became the answer. With confinement came the reservation, give them a piece of land and then due to gold, natural resources or whatever discovered on that land, take it back! The name "reservation" comes from the conception of the Native American tribes as independent sovereigns at the time the U.S. Constitution was ratified.

Change was blowing in the wind and at the time that Roosevelt became President, there were already 160 reservations with more than three hundred tribes represented. History will prove that from the Indian removal policy of 1830, to the forced assimilation peace policy of 1868 to the General Allotment Act of 1887 to create more reservations, it has been one congressional blunder after another. President Roosevelt to rectify these blunders wanted to appoint a Catholic to the Board of Indian Commissioners to reverse the pattern of discrimination. Once Archbishop Napoleon Joseph Perche got wind of this he felt that as if from divine intervention there was only one person right for the job. And indeed, that was Father Otto.

A relay of phone calls from the Archbishop to the Cardinal to His Holiness Pope Pius X made the request unanimous to the President of the United States. And indeed Fr. Otto became one of the commissioners on the Board of Indian Affairs.

No one ever feels adequate when called upon for a monumental task but the compassion that Fr. Otto felt for the American Indian more than made up for any of his political inadequacies. And with those sentiments, Fr. Otto was on his way to Washington, DC.

Washington, DC, is no place for amateurs, but Fr. Otto was learned, pugnacious and had the will of a fiery God on his side. And God had good reason to create us with free will so we had to choose whether to believe and trust in him. Fr. Otto already made that choice but now his free will chooses to help our neighbor. Those months that he spent with the Blackfoot Nation inspired him to fight to preserve a people's customs and traditions for a beautiful way of life. He had a full agenda of meeting senators, hearings with congress and dealing with the president's staff. Enthusiastic for the cause and energized to fight for what was right for a people that he loved, the month passed by quickly and the wedding date of Wolfgang and Mila arrived.

He had arranged to arrive in Memphis the day before the wedding and had a telegram sent to Big John Dawson back when he first learned about the wedding plans. The telegram urged Big John to find Running Bear and invited both families to the wedding.

The day of the wedding the bride looked beautiful as ever with her father ready to walk her down the aisle. Wolfgang and Steve his ring bearer were in the side room waiting for the wedding march to begin when the families of both Kurt and big John Dawson walk into the church. With smiles beaming and hugs a plenty, it was indeed a happy reunion as Father Otto proceeded with the wedding.

The ceremony of marriage is indeed a beautiful and happy occasion but what makes a crowd lively is a good old fashion hoedown. The fiddles and banjos come out and the foot stomping music begins with hoots, hollers and smiles. The hoopla even got Fr. Otto out on the dance floor with laughter from all as he wore himself out. Big John Dawson made the comment to Fr. Otto, "Do I need to get the mule to get you home, Father?"

There is such bliss when family and friends get together. The sharing, the laughter and especially the shear enjoyment of the interaction of their company makes one's heart realize that every day is a gift from God. Fr. Otto got the biggest kick from Spotted Owl and Red Wolf who are much older now, brought a breechclout to see if their Un'kl O would care to take a swim with them in the mighty Mississippi. He roared with laughter when he saw the loincloth and remembered the time when he could be just plain Un'kl O. It was Ralph Waldo Emerson who once said, "It is one of the blessings of old friends that you can be foolish with them."

Then meeting the fine sons of Big John Dawson, fine strapping lads from Longtail the oldest boy right on down the line to Bobcat their youngest, Fr. Otto enjoyed talking with each one and learning about their dreams and ambitions and especially enjoyed their poignant questions about God. No matter how skeptical their questions may appear, Fr. Otto wanted to implant the seed of a loving God that loved us enough to send His Son and show His mercy. It is never easy to make their belief plausible trying to explain the implausible.

Everyone enjoyed the music, food and the camaraderie throughout the afternoon as the night drew near and Fr. Otto grabbed both Kurt and Big John aside to discuss with them an important matter. After explaining his appointment as one of the commissioners for the board of Indian Affairs, he told them that he felt like a fish out of water and needed the help of the tribes for their relevant opinion on reservations.

"What better choices do we have?" asked a disturbed Kurt.

Big John added his advice, "We are both white men living with the Indians and have learned to love their customs and way of life!" Reflecting to regain his line of thought Big John continued, "Reservations are not the answer!"

Fr. Otto then said, "Therefore I am going back with you to talk to Brave Hawk and White Eagle and hopefully get some input and their influence upon other Indian tribes."

"What makes a great deal of sense is an Indian State where all tribes can live respectably together and in peace without any interference from Washington," an adamant Kurt proclaimed.

"Therefore, I need your help to get all the pros and cons on reservations before I go back to Washington." Fr. Otto continued, "Right now it is Washington's only solution to Indian affairs, reservations that confine and destroy a beautiful way of life."

With that having been said, each of them returned to enjoy family, friends and finish the day in good cheer.

Fr. Otto caught up with Stefan and asked him, "And will there be time for marriage and a family in your life?"

Stefan replied, "Living in a saddle from one town to another isn't much for family life, but I've been thinking of hanging up the badge and hanging out the shingle to start my law career."

"That sounds more promising than traveling the country as a U.S. Marshal," Fr. Otto told Stefan.

He continued by asking, "Where would you call home?"

"Well how about Memphis, this town is booming and is as good as any place especially with my brother staying here and starting his family," Stefan quickly replied.

The smoke stacks bellowed thick clouds of white smoke, the paddle wheels churned the mighty Mississippi waters and the boat's whistle echoed throughout the valley as the "Memphis Lady," a beautiful steam ship, meandered through the bends of the river. Wolfgang piloted the Memphis Lady along with his new wife at his side for what better way is there to start their honeymoon then to see a part of the country together with family and friends. It would be a few days up the Mississippi River before making the transit along the Missouri to Fort Benton. And yes, there was even a layover stop long enough for Un'kl O to put on his breechclout and jump in the river for a swim along with his nephews and Big John's sons and feel the giddiness of being a young child again. Moments in life like these are precious for the memories are held tenderly in our heart and mind forever. Embraces and fond farewells were given as Wolfgang and his wife proceeded back along the Missouri River from Fort Benton and the small band headed towards the Blackfoot camp. Both families, along with Fr. Otto, were eager to make the trek to the Indian camp.

The early nineteen hundred didn't only see the first Catholic on the Bureau of Indian Affairs which was part of the U.S. Department of the Interior but ushered in a new dawn of innovations as Henry Ford founded Ford Motor Company, the first successful flight by the Wright brothers in a mechanically propelled airplane, the first World Series where Boston defeated Pittsburgh and the first Olympics in the U.S. in St. Louis opened a new era of improvement in technology, medicine and culture. But through the millenniums of time the human struggle for different races to live together in peace seems to be mission impossible. It has always been a stalemate between the Indian culture and white culture concerning ownership of land with one resounding question from the Indian, "We were here first and this land is ours, so how did we lose our mother earth?"

One broken treaty after another led to formation of hostile renegades, violence and Indian wars and an uncompassionate Washington. Concerned over the impending attitudes and circumstances for a stalemate from both sides to work together, Fr. Otto wanted to bridge the differences for a feasible solution. It was indeed a bittersweet reunion for the tribe's people were happy to see Fr. Otto but disillusioned by the white man's government.

Brave Hawk asked, "We are a nomadic people for we follow the buffalo. Will your government keep the buffalo on the reservation?"

Fr. Otto understood the pain and hurt that Brave Hawk was feeling for he could empathize with him because he remembered all too well what it felt like to leave his homeland and family. He just bowed his head and nodded.

Brave Hawk continued with the soul-searching questions, "Mother Earth and her offspring the mountains, the forest and the streams are for our existence and we don't have all of that on reservations. The white man keeps coming to take our land, the buffalo disappear and our way of life dies!"

Just then White Eagle broke into the conversation and asked, "How can a God who created all, loves all, allow this to happen?"

White Eagle moved closer to Fr. Otto and gently placed his hands on his shoulders and with a deep penetrating stare called him by his Indian name, "Spirit Heart, the Great White Spirit and your God is one and the same God!"

Spirit Heart smiled and replied, "Yes, He is!"

White Eagle continued to ask, "Your people practice many religions and your government tolerates all of them, so why don't they tolerate ours?"

With a heavy heart, Spirit Heart looked at White Eagle and whispered, "I don't know."

"Then how can you possibly help us?" asked a sincere White Eagle.

It was just a matter of time before the Blackfoot People would be moved to a reservation and Fr. Otto felt the urgency for their loss. He prayed, sought counsel, and prepared to go back to Washington to rectify their plight but knew down deep that due to continual expansion west, the extermination of the buffalo and a greedy nation that wanted all the land; it was a helpless cause. Canada experienced the same plight and their answer was Indian reserves and so their migration crossing of a borderless continent would soon come to an end. The remainder of his time with the Blackfoot he enjoyed a loving people and a beautiful way of life that soon would be lost forever.

Brave Hawk and White Eagle once again asked Spirit Heart to join them in the council circle to smoke the calumet and then join in the tribal Indian dance. Indeed, he was honored to do so. The entire tribe witnessed the ceremony along with the families of Running Bear and Big John Dawson.

The following morning Brave Heart awoke early for White Eagle asked him to pray with him this one last time. They did not walk the path to the mountain but instead, to the surprise of Spirit Heart, journeyed a distance from the camp to the burial mound where a new scaffold had been erected. Once they arrived White Eagle turned to Spirit Heart and said, "I am an old man and have seen many seasons, many wars and many changes, but now my last journey will be to the 'happy hunting ground.' I am anxious to go to my Father in the sky to live again as we were intended to live."

The two men embraced, said a short prayer together, and then White Eagle ascended to the top of the burial scaffold. His last words to Spirit Heart were, "Go, my brother, and do what you can for if we are forced onto reservations then our way of life will decease forever."

With a heavy heart, Fr. Otto said his goodbyes and followed Big John to return home. At the beckoning of Brave Hawk, Fr. Otto did not proceed directly back to Washington but proceeded by steamboat back along the Missouri River accompanied by Big John to visit the brothers of the Blackfoot known as the Sioux. They are a deeply spiritual and proud people with a rich, beautiful heritage believing in a pervasive god, "Wakan Tanka," the Great Mystery. The Sioux are a confederacy of many tribes that speak three different dialects and spread east as far as Wisconsin, as far west as Montana and in-between throughout the Dakotas and Wyoming.

Big John had learned well the tongue of his brothers and led Fr. Otto to the Lakota camp also known as the Teton Sioux. The Sioux generally call themselves Lakota or Dakota meaning friends or allies and shared with both men their proud history and ancestral legends about the prairie dwellers for like the Blackfoot people they too were always on the move. As a migratory people, they asked Fr. Otto, "How can your government confine us on a reservation?"

He shared their food, smoked the calumet with them, and learned about the white settlers that continually keep coming and take their land. Multiple treaties are made and all are broken, hence the nickname for the white man as he who speaks with fork tongue. Then he learned of the major Indian wars, numerous battles and the skirmishes that gave the Indian a bad reputation as savages when defending their land, families and way of life. Patiently Fr. Otto listened and scribbled his notes to keep up as Big John interpreted their stories from the first major clash at Fort Laramie, Wyoming back in 1854 through the skirmishes and battle of Little Bighorn to the massacre at Wounded Knee in 1890. Even though there were literally hundreds of Indian Tribes throughout North America, the same stories could be repeated from every tribe, each in a different place and different time.

Upon his return to St. Louis, Fr. Otto boarded the train to Washington D.C. and reflected on the demise of the American Indian as he prepared his speech that he would present to congress. The day before the joint session of Congress President Roosevelt wanted a private meeting with Fr. Otto to learn just what he would say in his speech. He listened attentively, was courteous and reflected on every word.

Fr. Otto explained the Indian way of life, their mélange of customs, prayers, songs and traditions that would be lost forever due to no recorded history. Oral tradition is beautiful but doesn't preserve the quintessence of the Indian life. He understood how the Indian people wanted an independent Indian State and tried in vain to persuade the president the logic in the reasoning. This would bring peace and a definitive boundary for both sides. President Roosevelt stood up from his huge swivel chair, stared out from the oval office's arched windows and mused over the idea. Then he slowly turned towards Fr. Otto and replied, "Admirable but not pragmatic."

He paced throughout the office and then continued his line of thought by saying, "The American Indians are too factionalized, too divided to ever unify into one nation. There is no common language and no common trust to govern as one. This is what makes America great, all that diversity in race, religion and customs but able to unify as one to govern all. Even after a civil war that split us into two different ideologies and divided this great nation; we are united and stronger together once again."

Fr. Otto left the office completely frustrated and unsettled as to how to now address congress. Perplexed, he knew down deep that faith in One God was the same for both the American Native and American people but how can life prosper for one and not the other became a taunting enigma for him. He looked at the speech one more time and then crumbled it in his hands and tossed it away. When one is lost where does one turn but to the One that made all things possible. Fr. Otto needed a time in seclusion for prayer and to ponder his next move.

The next day when called forward to address congress, Fr. Otto arose from his seat and proceeded to the podium. All eyes were upon him as he started with the customary salutations and then proceeded to say, "There was a time when the land was sacred and the ancient ones were as one with the land.

> "Sunrise awakened them to the light of a new
> day,
> the prudence of wisdom to appreciate all of
> God's creation.
> The words of prayer are subtle and poignant
> to point the clear way,
> singing birds, furry creatures, blooming flow-
> ers show delightful appreciation.

Sturdy trees swaying, clouds moving across
the sky and snowflakes falling,
snow cap mountains, flowing streams with
forest and prairies to delight.
A summer's rain to quench the earth and cool
our thirst so nothing will die,
colorful leaves, a gentle cool breeze to fore-
warn of winter's call.
Clean white snow and shimmering delight of
the moon on a winter's night,
Seasons come and seasons go with the years
that seem to glide by,
shooting stars, planets aglow, and the aurora
borealis make quite a sight.
Bow thy head, say your grace and thank Him
for each passing night!"

Fr. Otto stared at the members of congress and gives them
a moment to contemplate what was just said. Then he asked
the question, "Are we not our brother's keeper?"

"Do we love our neighbor enough to do justice for them?"

Then after a moment of silence, he asked, "Do we consider the American Indian our neighbor?"

Growls and scowls could be heard and seen throughout
congress.

Fr. Otto maintained his composure and asked, "Is there a
better solution for the American Indian then the confinement

of the reservation, for if we confine them to the reservation today, then who tomorrow is doomed to internment?"

President Roosevelt looked about and under his breath said, "My God, I've seen people take the high road of the idealist and some the low road of the pragmatic, but very few take the moral path for truth."

With the passing months, the government realized that if the buffalo was the Indians' life supply, there was no way to force the Indians onto reservations. Decimation of the beast began at once and the reservations became a way of life. A dejected Fr. Otto finished his term on the commission and then returned to the religious life. President Theodore Roosevelt appointed Francis Leupp as Commissioner of Indian Affairs.

There are three qualities in life to keep us on the path of truth, reverence for God, respect for life and honor to uphold what is right. Whenever we shun reverence, respect and honor, then the moral decay for human kind begins and wrong choices are made.

Chapter 10
Logging, Mining, & Dams

The perverse bastards are fighting progress and Gus struggles with parliament to get the necessary laws passed to implement his energy reform bill. It is not in the human psyche to cooperate due to our biased nature. The political parties always yell for bipartisanship but the partisan bastards never cooperate. I swear that mankind has become the fickle fabric of frivolity. Gus has a deep trepidation about passage of the energy reform bill which is badly needed for Canada to move forward. Especially since so much time and effort has been invested to establish the logging camps for the Panama project, mining for the natural resources and engineering to build the dams and canals. Waterpower is vital to defray cost to generate the necessary electricity for enormous industry and manufacturing to boom if Canada wanted to stay competitive with the United States. And the canals were vital to open the Saint Lawrence Seaway for shipping. Gus has worked feverishly with surveyors, engineers and lawyers for months to combat the many hurdles to get this bill passed in parliament. As one engineer points out the astronomical cost estimate for just one dam causes Gus to slam his fist against the desk and exclaim, "Dam conundrums!"

Gus realized his dream to build nine canals throughout the Saint Lawrence Seaway and multiple dams for hydropower was too much to come to fruition in his lifetime. He ponders the dilemma and concedes to himself that the legacy for Canada will take many generations and decides to just start the dream. Looking over the figures Gus turns to look at the map to figure the site for one dam and the strategic location for one set of canals. Whenever a perplexing problem arose, Gus would light up his pipe and puff awhile to ponder his next move. Phillip Montangue, the head engineer of the project, explained to Gus that the horsepower potential is found by multiplying the water's flow measured in cubic feet per second by its height measured in feet. That the output of any hydroelectric plant to produce enough kilowatts needs a massive reservoir and a dam with enough height to create enough flow through the penstock to spin the turbine continuously. Gus didn't realize at the time that it would take another two decades to complete the Beauharnois Power and Seaway Canal. Just then his son, Lucas walks in with the legal papers for his dad to approve the necessary landsite for the dam by eminent domain.

"Dad, these papers need to be signed here and dated to move forward," Lucas explained as Wilhelm walked into the room.

"Gus, we got big problems looming about a strike in the northwest with one of our logging camps!"

A disturbed Gus spoke up and told Wilhelm, "There is no way that we can afford any work stoppages to meet our lumber quotas."

"I know," said a disgruntled Wilhelm.

"Well what is the problem now?" Gus retorted.

"No one seems to know, but a fear has spread throughout the camp and disrupted the work flow!"

Gus then asked, "What about the other logging camps, any problems there?"

"Not that I have heard and work is still progressing on all other campsites," Wilhelm added.

Gus pacing back and forth in his office finally told Wilhelm, "Well, I need to resolve this issue, find someone we trust to go out there and find out first-hand what the hell is the problem!"

Wilhelm told Gus, "I will personally go and find out what is causing the ruckus!"

Gus looked at his old friend and comrade admirably and remarked, "God Speed!"

Meanwhile Lucas waited impatiently for his dad to sign the legal documents needed to pre-empt land as Gus talks to the engineers about issues on the dam for the waterpower project. Gus concluded his business with the engineers and turns to his son to sign his life away.

"There signed, sealed, and delivered," said as he handed the pretentious affidavits to his son and encourages him to join me for dinner this evening.

"It seems that you have been avoiding your old man lately," Gus questioned his son.

Shaking his head Lucas replied, "Everything has been hectic dad and tonight will be fine for dinner!"

Gus pushed the issue further, "You mean business or pleasure?"

A despondent Lucas replied, "Life in general!"

With that, Lucas left the prestigious office of the minister of the interior and wondered if this was a good time to break some news to his father.

Quebec has a reputation for some of the finest restaurants and one of Gus' favorites was the, "Le Gout de la Vie," the taste of life, which served delectable food and wine in a private setting away from the crowd to enjoy the evening. The food was great and the conversation congenial until Gus mentioned, "Have you heard from your brother, Svante, recently? I understand that Olivia is ill and not doing too well and your nephew, Adam, is now a foreman at the shipyard in Bath, Maine?"

"No Father, Svante and I don't correspond these days," an apprehensive Lucas said while clearing his throat before continuing. "I'm afraid I let the cat out of the bag with Svante before saying anything to you."

Gus leaned forward and scrutinized the countenance of his son before asking, "What are you trying to tell me, son?"

"Father, I am gay; I am a homosexual!"

Gus sat back in his chair, took a sip of his drink and then smiled wryly and leaned forward again before saying, "You are my son, and I love you dearly. I will be the first to admit that I don't know whether homosexuality is innate or visceral, but this is what I feel and do know."

Gus sat back and took another drink and then continued, "It doesn't matter in life whether you are heterosexual or homosexual; there is still one God and one set of rules for life. We know them as the ten commandments and the beatitudes. The rest of life depends upon the choices we make."

An apprehensive Lucas began to regain his composure and replied, "I was afraid to tell you!"

"Son," Gus began to say, "there is no problem or moral dilemma with the orientation but the activity. And as far as I am concerned, whether heterosexual or homosexual, we are both in the same boat; our activities are accountable to Him above."

With that response, the path had been paved and they enjoyed the rest of the evening.

There are very few moments throughout life that are defining where a person's love, trust and values are tested. It can be climactic such as sacrificing one's life for another or supportive to give love and understanding or even conso-latory as in prayer and worship. Life's moments can be so poignant that these crossroads or intersections in our life are the impetus to achieve, change direction or accept our fate. Not all of life's questions are answerable in this life. For now, Gus needed to retire for the evening to reflect and pray.

The long train ride from Quebec to Calgary covered some 3,858 kilometers and plenty of time for reflection. Wilhelm just wished he had a better handle on the cause of the work stoppage to better prepare his countermeasures. But when one is oblivious to the magnitude of the problem, apprehension sets in which causes much anxiety for the du-ration of the trip. The delectable drink of Jack Daniels might have worked for Gus, but Wilhelm was a coffee drinker and the more he drank, the greater the anxiety de-veloped. A shorter train ride from Calgary to Prince George and a switch to the logging rail to make his destination to the Kwadacha Forest was a relief when logging camp 2736 came into view. Gabriel Crawford, logging manager, met Wilhelm as he disembarked from the train.

"Top of the morning to ya, Wilhelm!" he said as he ex-tended his arm for a handshake.

"Well, a top of the morning to you, Gabriel, I guess, for I have read your report about the work stoppage but don't really understand the reason why!"

Gabriel was cordial but all business as he said, "Let me get you situated in my cabin and then we can talk."

It was a short walk to his makeshift cabin and office and one could see some work going on but not much activity considering the size of the logging camp. There was a common dining hall where the old-time loggers ate at long tables stretching some thirty feet long and adjacent to the dining hall, four bunk houses, all stacked with double-bunk beds and tables to play cards. Across the yard there were the blacksmith shop where one could see the double-bladed axes, two-man saws, wedges and assorted tools needed for the job displayed in a rack, stables, company store, meat house with plenty of flies and storage sheds. Wilhelm couldn't help but notice jagged holes in the rooftops and sides of the buildings. Once inside the main office Gabriel set Wilhelm's luggage aside and went to the pot belly stove to pour each of them a cup of hot coffee.

While sipping his coffee, Wilhelm looked over the roster board posted on the north wall of the cabin on job assignments. Logging crews developed their own unique vocabulary, jargon like, "faller," a worker who felled trees, "bucker," workers who cut them into pieces, hauler and loader which is self-explanatory. Life in a logging camp is a daily battle for the survival of the fittest, whether man, beast or tree. From fatal accidents, wild beasts including bed bugs to unforgiving weather and the worst catastrophe of all, forest fires, it was a constant battle for all.

Wilhelm turned towards Gabriel and asked, "Alright, tell me what isn't in the report that you sent us?"

"Logging camp 2736 had a crew size of eight hundred men. We are down to about five hundred now. Many have left and more want to leave. Everything proceeded fine for the first two months and plenty of logging was accomplished. Then about two weeks ago, these strange howls through the night began which awoke most of the crew and keeps them up. The howling goes on for some three to four hours. This kept up for the first week and by the second week these creatures were hurling boulders about the size of grain sacks at the buildings. These damn boulders are twenty to thirty inches across tossed like baseballs. Hence all the holes in the walls and roof structures of the buildings. A few of the crew got smashed by a boulder causing a few broken bones but so far, no deaths. Then these huge hairy creatures start lugging off some of the men. Well, that was the last straw for most and that is when people started leaving! They are too afraid to stay."

Wilhelm, shaking his head, said, "That is the most damnable thing that I have ever heard!"

Gabriel stood up and said, "Well, I thought you might say that and to tell you the truth, I didn't believe it myself until I saw the whole tale unravel before my very eyes."

"Tonight, I am staying and want to witness the whole episode," an adamant Wilhelm claims, "and then we'll see where we go from that point. What time does the festivities begin?"

"The shenanigans begin around midnight," Gabriel claimed while setting up the bunk for Wilhelm.

It was a clear moon on a bright night as Wilhelm peered out the window and about midnight as if on cue, the howling began. The howling was much louder and deeper than any coyote and extremely annoying. Wilhelm could see why this cacophonous sound could drive the men crazy. Within a half hour the huge boulders came crashing upon the buildings.

"Damn," Wilhelm exclaimed, "this is ridiculous, where the hell is the shotgun?"

A disturbed Gabriel exclaimed, "I don't know what would happen if we killed one of those creatures!"

Wilhelm asked, "Have you ever seen one?"

"Yes, tomorrow I will show you some of their footprints in the ground and from that you may believe the rest of my story. But for now, no one ventures outside for they only come out at night," Gabriel explained.

Wilhelm still in disbelief as to what was happening just shook his head and asked, "Are there any other witnesses to these creatures?"

"Yes, many of the men have seen them and there is one of the loggers that survived their capture," Gabriel continued, "you may want to talk to him before he leaves the camp."

"Why is he leaving?" a disgruntled Wilhelm asked.

A frustrated Gabriel explained, "He along with a few others have had enough!"

"Well, let me talk to the men and if any of them are set on leaving, I'll arrange some compensation for each of them to help them out!"

The stone throwing ceased for the night and they turned in for some shut eye but Wilhelm was apprehensive about sleeping.

The next morning as the bell rang for breakfasts at 5 a.m. both men arose and got ready to start their day. Gabriel brought a tape measure and walked towards the perimeter of the logging camp with Wilhelm in pursuit. Upon coming on a set of footprints, Gabriel kneeled and measured the length of the footprint.

"Twenty inches long and nine inches wide with a stride of about ten feet!"

Wilhelm just pushed his hat to the back of his head and whistled, "Why, that creature is huge to make that kind of stride!"

"Yep," said Gabriel, "now you see why I waited till now to tell you that this creature is eight to nine feet tall and weighs in the range of 600 to 700 pounds."

"My God, why haven't we heard much about this creature before now?"

Gabriel replied, "Who would believe it?"

He continued, "There are legends and some folklore from some of the First Nation Tribes but no documentation to substantiate any of the claims."

A confounded Wilhelm asked, "Where do they come from?"

"Best I know, they have always been here and seem to be some remnant of the old cave man days that somehow continue to exist. The Indian tribes have co-existed in the Pacific

Northwest with these people. The Indians Nations call them Sasquatch and the white man calls them "Big Foot."

Wilhelm, laughing, said, "How appropriate judging from the size of those tracks!"

Wilhelm moved closer to the tracks and walks around the perimeter of the logging camp with Gabriel in close pursuit.

After making a once around the camp, Wilhelm concluded that there must have been at least twenty of the beast and told Gabriel that he would like to talk to any of the men that will voluntarily speak to him.

After a large, scrumptious breakfast, arrangements were made for the men to speak to Wilhelm before he addressed them on compensation for anyone that wants to leave and an increase in pay for anyone that stays.

One of the loggers yelled out, "Stop the ruckus, and we'll all stay!" which was followed by a round of cheers from the crew.

Gabriel turned to Wilhelm and asked, "What are you going to do?"

"Well," Wilhelm, scratching his head, began by saying, "I can't contact my boss and tell him that there are human-like giants who live deep within the forests that are ten feet tall, extremely powerful and have a terrible smell are howling and hurling stones at us! He would have me committed!"

Giving it some thought, Wilhelm finally explained, "I need to handle this myself and then when I go back to Quebec try to appease my boss why I spent so damn much money to resolve the issue!"

Looking at Gabriel apologetically, he then said, "I need someone that really knows these creatures and can help us to get rid of them! Any suggestions?"

"There is an engineering company known as the Dutchman Northwest Survey & Engineering that did the surveying throughout British Columbia for the rail lines to each logging camp. They had a guide known as Logobola from the Tsimshian Indian Tribe who used to tell us stories of such creatures. Perhaps he could help us!"

"Fine, that's just what I am looking for, how do we get in touch with him?" asked Wilhelm.

Over the next few days, Gabriel got in touch with the surveying company and communications relayed to Andrew Duncan about their problem and a request for Logobola's help. Two weeks had gone by without any word from either Andrew or the Dutchman Northwest Survey & Engineering Company. An exasperated Wilhelm went over to the mess hall for some coffee when he noticed a band of natives with wolf hounds coming towards the cabin. There had to be some thirty to forty Tsimshian Indians with about twenty hounds. Logobola led the band of natives and approached the cabin as Gabriel came out to greet them. After a short pow-wow and Wilhelm agreeing to the payment terms for their services, the band set up perimeter camps around the logging campsite some 200 feet out. At night, large bond fires were lit at each post with two to three Indians with a set of hounds standing guard. Each post was clearly visible around the entire logging camp to see if anyone tried to approach from the forest. This was the cure needed to stop the marauding Sasquatch from attacking the logging camp.

Relieved that the howling and stone throwing ceased and most of the men had gone back to work, a congenial Wilhelm paid compensation to the workers that wanted to leave.

There was one young man that Wilhelm took a special liking to from the old country of Sweden whose name was Albert. He was bright, ambitious and learned his trade of carpentry in the twin cities of Minnesota. Due to a loss of jobs in the USA, came west and tried his luck at logging. With money earned and the compensation pay-out he could go back to Wisconsin and try his luck at farming.

Wilhelm was curious just how much Logobola knew about the Sasquatch and asked him about his knowledge of the beast.

He told him that his cousin once lived with the creatures, in fact he domiciled with one and they had a son. To the surprise of Wilhelm, he asked Logobola what they called the boy?

He replied, "Smelly."

The train ride back to Quebec, now that the logging issue was resolved, was relaxing and peaceful. Everything was fine until Wilhelm reported back to work to an exasperated Gus who greeted him with, "You spent how much money?"

Wilhelm held up his arms to ease Gus' disposition and calmly said, "Sit down, my friend, and I'll tell you a tale of how I was awakened by the howl of a "Big Foot" who hurled huge boulders like a slap shot from a hockey puck!"

When Wilhelm finished his story, a bewildered Gus had finished his sixth Jack Daniels. I am not sure if Gus believed any of the gullible tale but seamen from the merchant marine used to say that all sea stories have some basis of truth to them!

Legal battles were looming in court, disgruntled protest groups were on the march and parliament was in caucus over the energy reform bill. The department of interior of natural resources felt like an octopus at times with each arm being pulled by a different group. The federal department abnegated the duties of mineral titles, mineral land uses, mine permits and record keeping to the provincial departments. This allowed the Federal department to oversee the occupational safety, health and legal matters dealing with mining. Gus was intrigued and fascinated with the whole basic industry of mining because mining produces the primary materials needed by all other industries. The metals which are obtained from ores are used in machinery and electrical equipment as well as in all structures of buildings and bridges.

The dawn of mankind started the process when during the Stone Age, man started digging in the earth for flint to make weapons, later-on learning to mine and shape copper. Through the centuries discovering how alloying copper and tin produced a stronger, more durable metal; human ingenuity never ceased but aspires forward to improve and make better. Along came the iron age and with the production of iron and steel ushered in the Industrial Revolution. Who knows but some day we will send people to the moon or some distant planet.

In the first half of the twentieth century, Canada emerged as a major producing nation of a wide range of minerals and base metals such as copper, lead, nickel and zinc. But troubles were brewing and something was afoul in Kootenay as Gus's old nemesis resurfaced.

Major General Smet came storming into Gus's office like a bat out of hell with some disturbing news. Ever since the assassination attempts on Canadian officials and his dad, Lucas took it upon himself with the BHA to form a group of infiltrators to spy upon known covert groups such as organized crime, especially since their eradication from Canada. It had been pleasant for the past few years with no foul-play activity from organized crime until three months ago, mishaps began to happen at some of the mining camps. It began in the Kootenay region of British Columbia at the Sudbury and Sullivan mines. Explosions occurred that at first-hand looked accidental. Then more unaccountable explosions and cave-ins at the Flin Flon and Sherridon mines of Manitoba occurred.

Walking right up to Gus' desk and placing a map right over all of his paper work that showed the mining locations throughout Canada MG Smet said, "One explosion is accidental, but four explosions is too coincidental! Our informants tell us that more are to occur but don't know where or when. But there is to be a big pow-wow of the crime bosses of all places here in Canada to decide their next steps."

"The audacity of those smug, belligerent bastards," an outraged Gus said as he stood up to look at the map. "How the hell are we to contain this, Canada is too large of a nation and we have too many mines to guard each one? And why now?"

"Confirmed word has it that organized crime still wants a foothold in Canada and is ready to try again," said MG Smet, "especially since the United States is beginning to crack down on organized crime."

An impervious Gus strutted around from his desk and told MG Smet in no uncertain terms to "Get that information at any cost!"

Atrocious circumstances demand expedient solutions and Gus didn't want organized crime back into Canada under any circumstances. Gus turned and smashed his fist on top of his desk as he said, "Organized Crime is like a cancer, if not contained it spreads like wild fire while they mastermind their crime, manipulate the system and massacre their opposition."

Turning towards Lucas and MG Smet, Gus barked out the order, "Gentlemen, we are at war with organized crime!"

As they adjourned from Gus's office, both men understood their challenges and knew exactly what needed to be done. Lucas orders MG Smet to find the leak and get the necessary information before another atrocity occurs in Canada.

The reins needed to be tightened to stop the influx of crime before infamy triumphs. Within two weeks, MG Smet had the information needed to move on the crime bosses.

Alberta's Canadian Rocky Mountains are legendary for their snow cap mountains and lodges of hospitality beckoning all to come and enjoy. There was one such lodge near Castle Mountain renowned for its beautiful scenery and abundant snowfall. This reliable information as to where and when the meeting of the masterminds of organized crime were to meet came into their hands through a deeply entrenched informant.

The Dons were ahead of the crime families at which there were five families in the United States fighting amongst themselves for new territory. The Generals who were next in line and reported to the Dons kept the troops in order and were responsible for expanding the territory. There were two Generals located in the Chicago area and one of them was itching to expand into Canada. Reporting to the Generals were the Bishops responsible for handling the menial tasks of running the activities of drug trafficking, arms smuggling, financial crime and assassinations. Organized crime syndicates generate large amounts of money but the funds are of little valve to them unless the they can disguise the funds and convert it into legitimate investment enterprises. Hence, the interest in the legitimate mining of Canada. It is essential for the survival of organized crime to hide the money's illegal origin. Intricate money laundering schemes to wash cycle the money and convert the funds into usable assets requires a three-fold process of placement or immersion of the funds in small amounts at a time to avoid suspicion along with segmentation to disguise the trail to foil hot pursuit. Then after layering the funds to cover their trail, integration known by organized crime as spin dry to synthesize the funds into clean taxable income by real-estate transactions or sham loans.

The Knights who reported to the Bishops utilized the pawns or troops to carry out the dirty work and covert activities. The difficulty for law and order to combat organized crime is that their territory is like a chess board with organized crime always making the first move and always being a move ahead. The layered organization made it difficult for the wheels of justice to connect the crime committed directly back to the dons; for the Dons, crime did pay!

The powers in charge of the BHA were in a heavy meeting and were determined to stop organized crime from racketeering through extortion in Canada by any means necessary. It was damn cold throughout Canada and with record snowfall that year the BHA decided to use it towards their advantage.

The conceived plan was simple and the execution had to look like an accident to the rest of the world without any collateral damage. The BHA had five days to coordinate the plan and set the ambush. Paradise Ski Resort was a beautiful get-a-way with a main lodge with dining facilities, shops and a large lounge for nightly entertainment with four remote conference centers for privacy. Under the assumed name of Lindfield Transportation, organized crime reserved the Caribou Lodge for the three dons and their entourage.

On a cold winters day of January 22, 1905, the dons arrived at the Paradise Resort to enjoy what they thought would be a peaceful meeting to chart their plans for extortion of businesses throughout Canada. Present at the meeting were Don De Luca from the ancient district of Basilicata, Italy with his general Rossi, who enjoyed putting a man's arm in a meat grinder; Don Giordano from Messina with his general Bruno who maintained order by cutting off a man's genitals and watching him bleed to death while he ate his supper and finally Don Morretti from Catania, Sicily with his general Lombardi, who liked to use a stiletto to carve out a man's eyes. The louder the victim yelled, the deeper Lombardi would carve. There wasn't a man amongst the families that didn't fear Lombardi for his love of butchery and carnage of all his victims. The dons

along with their entourage were an ensemble of the most notorious, wretched bastards on the face of the earth! The following day, the meeting convened at 10am with Don De Luca
beginning the meeting with a toast to new ventures in Canada
and as he turned the meeting over to his counselor to format
the scheme, a map of Canada showing locations of major
mines was hung on the wall along with a list of targets for either bribery or assassination. At precisely 10:45 am six military transport trucks, camouflaged as construction vehicles
with "Obusier Construction" stenciled on the sides arrived to
the north and south end of the Caribou Lodge. Thanks to
Mack Trucks, Inc. which was founded in 1900 in Brooklyn,
New York, the Canadian government purchased the Mack
AC model to transport equipment. Each truck towed a howitzer with a firing range of 1400 yards. Three trucks to the
north and three trucks to the south of the lodge positioned
their howitzers. With a record snowfall of twenty-eight feet
and snow drifts of better than forty feet each howitzer was
positioned to fire upon the mountain range overshadowing
Caribou Lodge. At 11 am a thunderous roar echoed throughout the mountain range causing one gigantic avalanche to
come crashing down upon the Caribou Lodge. Authorities of
the BHA and North West Mountie Police posted off the area
and took two weeks to begin the process to recover bodies.
The illicit campaign for organized crime to infiltrate Canada
ended abruptly. Obusier Construction, French for Howitzer
Construction, was never seen or heard of again.

Lucas was a pundit of history and learned the lessons of war well by reading everything he could from Alexander the Great, to Napoléon and was an avid chess player. Know thy enemy or as the French would say, *"Demarche et De-marche!* Move and Countermove."* The BHA had now made their definite countermove. Only time would reveal what the next move would be for organized crime.

Chapter 11
Heaven's Gate

"Please God come to my assistance, oh Lord, make haste to help me!"

Father Otto was in deep prayer and meditation for he was greatly troubled about the present times.

"Heavenly Father I come to you on my knees to seek, to ask and to knock, that you animate within my heart and soul, a true desire to serve and help those less fortunate in life. Grant your unworthy servant the strength to be firm and the courage to do your will! I make this request through Jesus Christ, my lord and savior, Amen!"

Prayer and the sacraments provide moments where God can touch our lives in a special way that affords us the opportunities to grow in our relationship with God. The trouble for most of us is that we stop praying, seeking and asking. If we stop knocking, then the door will not be opened. When we say "Amen" to the lord, we are saying, "Yes, Lord, I do believe in you, let your will be done!"

As time passes, Fr. Otto spends more time in prayer, meditation and lectio divina. Archbishop Perche, cognizant of Fr. Otto's passionate zeal, also spends much time in prayer that the holy spirit would sustain and nurture Fr. Otto for his future endeavors. God always hears and discerns our prayers, but he will answer our prayers on His time schedule and not ours. It is important for us to realize that in the spectrum of eternity, time is of no consequence. One must always remember to continuously persevere and knock and then the door will be opened.

The core values of reverence, respect and honor were being lost in a sea of turmoil around the world for in 1905 French law enforced separation of church and state, the massive Russo-Japanese War began which culminated with more than 100,000 deaths in the largest world battles of this era. Canada passed a law that prohibited poor people from entering their country for any reason. As far as America, the average life expectancy was 47 years, the average wage in the U.S. is 22 cents per hour so the average worker made between $200 and $400 dollars per year. More than 95% of all births in the U.S. took place at home. The American flag has 45 stars. Only 6 percent of all Americans are graduating from high school.

The circumstances and pressures of life coerce some to make wrong choices while in other people it will necessitate the impulse to do right. Fighting, murder, suicide, drugs and divorce verses peace, life, forbearance and togetherness to uphold the core values for the tug of war between good and evil never ceases. Archbishop Perche and Fr. Otto realizes this so well as they both reflect and pray the Serenity Prayer:

God grant me the serenity to accept the things
I cannot change,
Courage to change the things I can,
And wisdom to know the difference. Amen

The scars of life should teach us caution and forbearance to persevere as we gaze upon our model in life, our lord, who carried his cross and fell-down not once, nor twice but three times. And what did he do? He picked himself up not once or twice but each time to persevere! This is what each of us must do in life! Our good life is one inspired by His love and guided by His knowledge as we are told, "I am with you always!"

Archbishop Perche reflects on the pillars of civilization and knows that these pillars help us in this life but do nothing to inspire us towards eternal life. Even the pillar of organized religion has faltered at times as it went through the crusades, inquisitions and reformation. He ponders that maybe he made a mistake of recommending Fr. Otto to be on the commission of Indian affairs for the struggles of government and religion don't mix well and the effects of that struggle have devastated Fr. Otto. Time is always at the essence and Archbishop Perche wanted to give some solace to Fr. Otto but didn't know where to begin and so turned to more prayer. In God's vision, there are only two types of people; those who believe and do his will and those who don't. In solitude, there are two outcomes, we either seek counsel in prayer and rise above the occasion or we withdraw within ourselves and deteriorate into disillusionment.

Archbishop Perche stayed in touch with God through prayer to receive some enlightenment, and now he could stay in touch with his colleagues with that great invention, the telephone. After conferring with several of his colleagues, a meeting was arranged at the diocese of Detroit to do some spiritual brainstorming.

The Great Lakes region of North America is a bi-national Canadian-American region that includes eight U.S. states as well as the Canadian province of Ontario. In the 1900s the Catholic population was better than 10 million, under the hierarchy of 14 Archbishops including two from Canada. Catholics were heavily concentrated in the industrial and mining centers of the Northeast, few were farmers and only a small fraction lived in the South, chiefly in Louisiana. At that period, there weren't any formalized meetings of the nation's bishops and so an impromptu meeting was called by the Archbishops. At that meeting the spiritual needs were discussed about:

- Laity
- Church
- Indian Nations
- Spiritus Dei

Especially the last category of how to bring the Spirit of God to all was of utmost importance. Through the discussions, prayers and worship during the three-day meeting, Archbishop Perche learned that a sizable acreage of farmland was donated to the church in the Chippewa county of the upper peninsula of Michigan. The donation came with a sizable grant of funds to do with the land as the church saw fit. The farmland with an apple orchard along the western slopes boarded along the shores of Lake Superior and had a sizable farmhouse on a hill overlooking the Tahquamenon Bay. There was a small island about fifty feet in diameter close to the shore that was greeted every beautiful morning by the sunrise. A haven in the wilderness where the river runs over a waterfall and empties into the cool waters of Lake Superior that gives a serene picture of grace and peace touched by the hand of God. The unanimous opinion amongst the archbishops was a delightful spot for a retreat house but whom shalt be put in charge of such an establishment? The wheels of his conscious mind were already turning but he didn't want to make the same mistake twice, as Archbishop Perche reflected on the name of Fr. Otto. Well respected amongst his peers, Archbishop Perche was received well by the other archbishops and encouraged for his recommendations. He expressed that indeed he had a good candidate in mind but would want to discuss the opportunity with the person before divulging his name.

There was much time for reflection and prayer as Archbishop Perche made the transit by train back to New Orleans. Upon his return, he made an impromptu visit to Fr. Otto and broke the news about the idea of a retreat house in the upper peninsula of Michigan. Fr. Otto being elated with the news informed the Archbishop that through much reflection and prayer, he too had some guidance from above to start a religious order of oblates of priests, brothers and laity to help the needy and wanted to call the religious order, "The Oblates of the Hands of Christ." Indeed, Archbishop Perche was overwhelmed and inspired for their prayers have seemed to be answered.

Major decisions should never be taken lightly but a special retreat for Fr. Otto was absolutely in order. Arrangements were made for Fr. Otto to spend a four-week retreat at St. Gregory's Monastery in Shawnee, Oklahoma which was founded in 1875. A Benedictine house of God for the individual to do some deep soul searching for the will of God through the daily Horarium of the Divine Office. The prophet says, "Seven times a day have I given praise to thee." In a Benedictine Monastery, they observe the sacred number of seven by observing and fulfilling the duties of service in the hours of Lauds, Prime, Terce, Sext, None,

Vespers and Compline. Archbishop Perche felt that the spirit would indeed lead Fr. Otto down the path of discernment to God for to oversee a retreat house is one avenue but the inception of a new religious order requires approval from not only his bishop but from His Holiness the Pope from Rome. The only concern should be the discernment of God's will for once the spirit leads then the mundane details will fall into place. And through the next several months the Holy Spirit consummated the zeal of Fr. Otto for there was much activity in the Chippewa County of Michigan.

The entrance gate to the retreat house read, "Heaven's Gate, A welcome refuge for all souls."

The existing farmhouse became a rectory with the additions of two wings, one for the newly founded order of "Oblates of the hands of Christ" and the other for guest.

A church was built with a cloister for reflection and prayer with a pathway that meandered through the grounds by the waterfall and to the covered bridge that crossed-over to the island. A sign placed above the covered bridge read in both English and Lakota, "Wakan Tanka Kici Un," which means, "May God Bless." The huge wooden door to the church had a life size carving of Jesus Christ with both of his hands extended to welcome all newcomers. One had to open the door by touching the hands of Christ. Above the door were the words, "You Touch My Hands to Open the Door and I will Touch your Heart to Open Your Soul."

The healing touch of faith can renew a broken person for everyone has been wounded at one time or another by the arrows and spears of life and the need for everlasting love is real. Word spread far and wide about the retreat house and many people started to come which was no easy trek. There were no bridges to the upper peninsula of Michigan and the horse and cart was still the major mode of transportation even though the advent of the automobile had begun. The only way to reach the retreat house was by car ferry across the bay of Lake Michigan or the long trek through Wisconsin to the UP. For those that came, the reward far out-weighed the hardships of the trip. Mayhem, death and atrocities have affected everyone at one time or another as we go through life and the only help is spiritual solace. Whether we instigate the sin or the sin is laid upon us by another, the burden of the sin causes the weight of our cross and dampens the path to salvation. Fr. Otto realized that no two people were alike in seeking spiritual solace and so designed the healing process differently for each person that came to Heaven's Gate but included eight major steps:

- Path of Solace
- Prayer
- Divine Reading
- Meditation / Reflection
- Contemplation / Listening through the Heart & Soul

- Worship
- Penance
- Steps of Healing

One of Fr. Otto's first participants to the retreat house was a Bishop who served the Diocese of Superior in Wisconsin. The oldest Catholic congregation in the state of Wisconsin is the Diocese of Superior which was started in July 27, 1836 by a Fr. Frederic Baraga who arrived at La Pointe and immediately set to work, building a log church. A Jesuit missionary who had much success evangelizing the native people and early European immigrants. Now, Bishop Augustine Albert Schwinn worked diligently to grow many priests from ten to sixty along with five mistresses for the long winter evenings. A spiritual cleansing was needed as he came to Heaven's Gate and approached Fr. Otto to go through the eight-step process of healing the soul.

The healing process of the soul is a difficult journey for one must be open and honest with themselves and God. No stone must be left unturned and requires a sincerity to rid the compunction.

Fr. Otto walked with Bishop Augustine along the path of solace and sensed that he had a deep secret within that he must get rid of if he was ever to make a good retreat. As they come to a small clearing, there were three huge crosses, reminding any participant that Jesus Christ died for all of us. Fr. Otto turned to the Bishop and pointed to the three crosses and quoted from the Gospel of Matthew, "Whoever exalts himself will be humbled; but whoever humbles himself will be exalted." He allowed a few moments to reflect on the words and then said, "Woe to you, scribes and Pharisees, you hypocrites. You are like white-washed tombs, which appear beautiful on the outside, but inside are full of dead men's bones and every kind of filth. Even so, on the outside you appear righteous, but inside you are filled with hypocrisy and evildoing."

His laconic words penetrated like a dagger and left the bishop's countenance looking a pasty white as he had to sit down on a bench near the pathway. Fr. Otto took out his stole and sat on the bench next to him and then said, "This is as good a time to begin penance!"

The bishop got on his knees and began with, "Bless me Father for I have sinned," and began telling of his sins.

"I have had five mistresses, one for each season."

Fr. Otto interrupted the bishop and said, "But there are only four seasons!"

The bishop replied, "Yes, Father, it was a very merry, merry Christmas."

Once the bishop concluded his confession, Fr. Otto reminded the bishop of the words of St. John Chrysostom who said, "The road to hell is paved with the skulls of erring priests, with bishops as their signposts." And then told the Bishop that his absolution is contingent on getting rid of the five mistresses. That as his penance, he wanted the bishop to reflect on the words of St. John Chrysostom, say his daily prayers and meditate with Christ on why he became a priest. Then he said to him, "Turn to Christ our Lord and Savior and he will guide you and give you rest!"

Through the remainder of the retreat, Fr. Otto saw a gradual transformation in the bishop from being cavalier, to somber and finally a happy individual. He had been reenergized in his worshiping and appeared ready to take the final steps of healing.

On the last day of the retreat, Fr. Otto arose before sunrise, awakened the bishop and together walked to the covered bridge. He instructed the Bishop to follow the engraved stones and reflect on each one and as he walks around the island, come to a major decision on how he is to change his life before exiting the covered bridge.

Bishop Schwinn walked across the covered bridge and reflects on the words, "May God Bless," posted over the bridge. He thought to himself, *can God bless a worthless sinner like me?* He came to the first engraved stone in the ground which read, "I am the way, the truth and the life," with an arrow pointing towards the east. He thought to himself, *your ways, dear Lord, are always truthful but my ways haven't always been truthful.* He walked along the path slowly towards a bench as the sunrise peaks over the horizon. Another engraved stone in front of the bench, which was facing east, read in Latin, "Creatio ex nihilo, et erit lux," which means, creation from nothing, let there be light.

The Bishop sat on the bench and watches the sunrise. The warmth felt good as he sat there with his eyes closed, reflecting on the words of Jesus Christ, that he is the light of life. The passions in his heart set the tone for the stirred emotions within him. He sat there for some time in solitude and prayer. Eventually he rose and followed the path that led him to another bench and stone, which was engraved with the words, "I came to reveal the Father, to teach, to touch and to heal!" Bishop Schwinn looked back over his life and asked himself, "Have I been a good priest, a good bishop," and stops to ponder, "a good Shepard?" In due time, he continued his journey of self-discovery and proceeds to the last bench facing west and read the engraved stone, "I died for you!" Bishop Schwinn covered his face with both hands, fell to his knees and wept. The stains of our own sins can be too much to bear at times, just imagine carrying the sins of the world. Now he proceeded back to the covered bridge and for the first time looked up and noticed the sign going back across the bridge, "I am with you always." The true hope in our life.

He went directly back to his religious cell and opened his suitcase and looked for his mitre before heading back to the covered bridge. Along each side of the covered bridge there was a shelf to leave an artifact symbolizing a change in one's life. Fr. Schwinn had decided to resign from his position and seek entrance to the Oblates of the hands of Christ as he leaves the mitre on the shelf. As the

Bishop prepared to leave the retreat house to travel back to his diocese, Fr. Otto reflected on the words of Christ in the Gospel of John which says, "Amen, Amen, I say to you, unless a grain of wheat falls to the ground and dies, it remains just a grain of wheat; but if it dies, it produces much fruit." Hopefully the choices that Bishop Schwinn made now will bear much fruit.

The seasons passed; many artifacts accumulated on the covered bridge, the participants' belief in God was bolstered and many continued to walk by faith as they left the retreat house. The community grew in spirit for now there were eight priest, including one ex-bishop, four brothers and six laity that administered to the needy. One of the main works of the Oblates of the hands of Christ was pastoral ministry for no request would be denied. One request came in from the Indiana's criminal justice system to administer last rites to death-row inmates. Indiana's capital punishment statue originally became law in 1897, and in the early 1900s individuals were executed by hanging. Comfort was sort for the criminal and comfort was given as the Oblate would read the comforting words from the Bible of the insurgents hung on a cross, one to His right and one to His left as one of the criminals asked Jesus, "Remember me when you come into your kingdom." And Jesus replied, "Amen, I say to you, today you will be with me in Paradise." Life is a beautiful gift but life is also a mystery to be unraveled of Christ's unending love and mercy through each person to one another. Each of us are called, each of us have choices to make.

The first known inhabitants of the Upper Peninsula were tribes speaking Algonquian languages. The L'Anse Indian Reservation of the Lake Superior Band of Chippewa Indians was in Baraga County of the UP. Pastoral ministry needed at the reservation was provided by the Oblates of the hands of Christ. And as the pastoral needs of the communities grew so did the cost of funding those needs grow.

One morning Fr. Otto was delivering his homily and wasn't quite sure how to ask for an extra collection as he addressed the congregation and said, "I have some good news and some bad news. The good news is that we have the extra funds needed for our pastoral needs. The bad news is that the funds are still in your saddle bags!" With a little wit, Fr. Otto managed to raise the funds needed.

There are many twist and turns in life and some curves thrown to test our perseverance in faith. Some are beautiful and awe-inspiring as the birth of two babes, twins, a boy and a girl to Wolfgang and Mila and the request for Fr. Otto to do the Baptisms. A letter of the most joyous news and the anticipation to see them again and perform a glorious baptism. Fr. Otto looks at his calendar and quickly puts his pen to paper to give an affirmative to their request. But there was also word from his other brother, Kurt or should I say Running Bear, that brought devastating news of the death of Song Bird. A fatal accident from a catastrophic storm that hit Montana in the spring. His thoughts floated back to a happier time when he first met the family and their sons Spotted Owl and Red Wolf. A smile came over his face as he thought back of swimming with them and the loincloth until the bell rang for noon prayer which snapped his mind back to reality.

Letters and news from afar are fine but what gives a boost to life are those impromptu visits of smiles and hugs to perk up a man's soul from family and good friends. After noon prayer as the community adjourned for lunch, there was a visitor at the front door. Stefan was all smiles as he eyed his brother Otto coming towards the door. The glass window in the door framed his brother well for he could see the change in Fr. Otto's hair turning a grayish white. Time has moved on and it has been too long since they have last seen each other. Opening the refectory door, Fr. Otto said, "Top of the afternoon, Stefan," as he hugged his brother and beckoned him to come in. He graciously escorted him to the dining hall for some lunch and then afterwards, they walked around Heaven's Gate. This was Stefan's first visit to Heaven's Gate and as he broke the worldly news to his brother, he asked just as many questions about the retreat house.

Stefan looked at his brother Otto and said, "It is good to see you, brother, and how are you contending with life in the UP?"

"As fair as ever, life has been good!" replied Fr. Otto as they walked along the path and came to the waterfall.

"And what is the purpose of Heaven's Gate?" a quizzical Stefan asked.

"Well, my brother, there are many broken hearts, lost souls in this world that need help to find their way back and this is a place to help them find it."

They walked a little way and stopped to gaze out at the waterfall before Fr. Otto continued, "You see this path symbolizes the path of life, that we encounter many consequences in life, some good, some bad, some intricate and some definitely obstacles. One of the first encounters in life is baptism as infants, and I'm afraid that in many cases; it is taken too lightly. We receive in baptism the gifts of the Holy Spirit and our initiation to the faith. Through those gifts, it helps us to persevere and do God's will but very few are nurtured in their faith."

Stefan interrupted his brother and asked, "How do you know that?"

Fr. Otto smiled and replied, "Just look around you and see all the chaos, mayhem and unpleasantness, if people lived their holy gifts then we would see and feel the fruits of the spirit."

A frown came over Stefan's countenance as he asked, "I'm not sure and it is embarrassing to ask, what are the fruits of the Holy Spirit?"

Fr. Otto was happy to accommodate his brother by replying, "Remember when you were a child and you learned of love, joy, peace, patience, kindness, generosity, faithfulness, gentleness, and self-control? The greatest of these being love for the effects of the Holy Spirit active in human life is a two-way street. We receive these gifts but we must use them in our lives."

"I'm afraid in my line of work as a U.S. Marshall and now as a lawyer, I don't see much of the effects of the Holy Spirit in life."

"Then you begin, my brother, and you do some good so others can see the gifts through you!"

Stefan shook his head in the affirmative as they walk towards the covered bridge. They stopped long enough to look up at the words engraved on the bridge and then proceed to cross the bridge as Stefan notices all the artifacts.

"What are all these articles left on the bridge for?"

Fr. Otto turned and looked at his brother solemnly as he tells him, "Contrition, a change of heart and contrition is not simply an individual act but a lifelong process."

Stefan pointed to one article with a frown on his face as Fr. Otto smiles and said, "An atheist who became a believer."

Stefan continued, pointing to the articles as he pointed to the Mitre, and Fr. Otto responded, "A bishop that resigned his position."

Stefan shakes his head, as his eyes scans over the different articles.

"You see this bridge symbolizes the bridge of life, for God sent His Son to be the bridge person to reveal what was invisible to us through Jesus Christ and now we must make the decision to cross over and decide to accept Christ as our Lord and Savior!"

Stefan was a little shaken-up and walked over to a bench to be seated and was silent for a while as he contemplated all that his brother has said. Then he looked up towards his brother and said, "I'm afraid that I have taken all of this for granted and am not quite sure where I stand with the Lord."

Fr. Otto smiled at his brother and said, "That's why I became a priest! Let me help you."

Stefan remained at the retreat house for three more days and it was good to see his brother. But even more so to be reintroduced to his faith and by the encouragement of his brother, Stefan went to confession with one of the other priest as Fr. Otto told him, "Let it all out, I won't know a thing."

Confession is good for the soul and talking to family is good for the heart as the two brothers got close again and Stefan explained his original purpose for the impromptu visit.

"I am going to be married, and I would like you to do the honors!"

Brotherly hugs were few and too far in-between as Fr. Otto hugged his brother and told him that it would be a pleasure and honor to marry them and asked, "Who is the lucky bride?"

"Her name is Rosalind, Rosalind Bauer."

Fr. Otto asked, "Why does that name sound familiar?"

"She is Mila's sister, remember, brother, Mila Bauer; has it been that long that you forgot our brother's wedding?"

They both laughed, cherished those precious moments of brotherly togetherness and before you know it, time was of the essence to leave. A future date was set for the wedding and Fr. Otto thanked God for His blessings as Stefan returned home.

Chapter 12
Sunrise Brings Another Day

"Faith is to believe what you do not see; the reward of this faith is to see what you believe." The words of Saint Augustine reverberated in Fr. Otto's mind and surged in his heart as the Oblates of the hands of Christ multiplied in number and became many helping hands of Christ throughout the parishes and Indian reservations of the United States and Canada. An injustice to any one race is an injustice to all of humanity, for we are all God's children. Fr. Otto felt that with God's guidance he could help all peoples through the religious order for he was still feeling the ill effects of his failure on the Indian Commission. Sometimes a thorn in the side can be a positive impetus to try different avenues to accomplish some good. The reputation of the order for accomplishing some good spread far and wide and the retreat house became famed for helping the lost. The Oblates wore a distinctive garb of a burgundy top which signified the blood of Christ with the embroidery of a small cross on the left side over the heart and a symbol of the sun on the right side for the light of Christ.

Gus and Wilhelm had been working diligently to get ready for one of the first energy consortiums that was to be held in San Francisco that year with attendance from many of the developed nations. Population growth, booming cities, financial innovations and the industrial revolution caused the demand for energy to zoom. The demands never stop but explode exponentially, and the cycle hastens in time to cause much anxiety. Gus hadn't been feeling well but thought it was just the long hours as he collapsed one day in the office. Due to a massive heart attack, Gus couldn't make the consortium but sent Wilhelm to shoulder the burden of the meeting. And once again Wilhelm found himself on those long, dull train rides that made him contemplate retirement. Wilhelm was already in his seventies and felt that this would be his last trip as he looked over his notes to polish off his speech. A speech that he never gave because in April of 1906, San Francisco experienced one of the worst earthquakes that mankind has ever seen in the United States; an earthquake which caused more than 3,000 deaths including the life of Wilhelm Axelson. The devastation from the loss of his good friend and the many years without his wife Elsa caused Gus to deteriorate and never recuperate from his heart attack. Gus was partially paralyzed now on his left side and lived with his son Lucas. The struggles in a wheelchair caused much frustration for Gus and with a growing concern for his dad's mental health, Lucas encouraged him to consider a spiritual retreat. The paradox to life is that there are three facets to our life, mental, physical and spiritual; the most important one being spiritual but it seems that we put the least amount of time on.

The pressing needs of the BHA are demanding on Lucas as he goes through his daily briefings on current events. It seems that his nemesis is still trying to gain a foothold into Canada as Major General Smet forewarns Lucas that precautions are of the utmost importance concerning organized crime. Organized crime has always been about power and money and if the bribe and the buck is their god; crime will always exist. Law and justice struggles as the pendulum swings from one side as governments strive to be proactive with new laws and then swings to the other side with criminals circumventing all the laws. Lucas decided right then and there to make the spiritual retreat with his father. He made all arrangements for their travel and after researching the various retreat houses decides on none other than the retreat house of the Oblates of the hands of Christ.

The train ride from Quebec to Detroit was a pleasurable journey with Lucas and his dad playing a few hands of cribbage which they hadn't done for years.

"Let's see now," Gus started to count his hand of, "fifteen two, four, six, with a double run of fours and a pair for a sixteen hand."

Lucas just smiled at his father's good fortune as he continued the count with the crib for another ten hand for a total of twenty-six points.

There was a transfer in Detroit for the train to Mackinaw City and then a short ride across the straits by ferry that took them to the upper peninsula. One of the first model cars, a curved-dashed Oldsmobile from Heaven's Gate accommodated them to the retreat house. As Lucas helped his dad into the wheelchair, Fr. Otto came out to warmly greet them to Heaven's Gate.

"May God Bless and welcome to Heaven's Gate; I am Fr. Otto!"

The first day at any retreat house is rather awkward for most to adjust to the total silence, seclusion, continual prayer and worship. By the second day the Horarium influences any open and sincere heart. On the third day, the words of the psalmist begin to penetrate and is absorbed by the heart, mind and soul. It's not until the fourth day that a transformation, a rebirth begins to unravel our secular ways and as the sages of old knew that it was necessary to withdraw from the world and seek what is above before a renaissance of the spirit can take place.

Fr. Otto leads them to the church, where one must touch the hands of Christ to open the door. Every person that comes to the retreat house whether pious or cynical is affected by touching the carving. Lucas pushed the wheelchair and had his dad open the door. They were led to a side room of the church and after a short prayer, Fr. Otto began the talk on God's Grace. He handed a paper to each one that read:

God's Grace
Go to God daily in prayer
Read God's word in the Bible
Accept His Will
Christ is the way, truth and life; He is our light
Eternal Life, follow Him and eternal life is our reward

Fr. Otto explained that each of us in our daily lives needs to speak to god, that he is always there to listen to us. It doesn't have to be as dramatic as the agony in the garden on the night before his death when Jesus spoke to his heavenly father, but He is always there in the good times and bad to listen to us. Read His word in the Bible and receive the breath of life. Accept His will for it is forever. Believe, dream, do some good and walk humbly with God as the prophet tells us.

Just then Gus looked at Fr. Otto and asked, "What is God's will?"

Fr. Otto smiled and replied, "We don't have to look any further than the ten commandments."

He paused just long enough for both Gus and Lucas to digest what he had just said before continuing, "They are as relevant today as the day He gave them to Moses."

"Remember it takes strength to love, but it takes courage to be loved," Fr. Otto again paused to allow them to reflect on those words.

Then he continued by saying, "Fidelity to God means fidelity to his laws and His Son."

Fr. Otto looked out through the stain glass window from the church and then looks back towards Gus and Lucas before saying, "Everyone is afraid at times in our life, just look at the life of Peter, from his call to discipleship to his eventual martyrdom in Rome. This is the person that Jesus said to him, you are rock and upon you I will build my church and yet he was so afraid, that he denied Jesus three times!"

At this point, Fr. Otto remained silent and allowed some reflection time. The sun was shining and the rays of sunbeams penetrate through the stain glass windows. Hopefully Fr. Otto's words were penetrating through their hearts and very soul.

Eventually Fr. Otto broke the silence and told them, "Come to know, love and follow Jesus for he is the way, the truth and life. In this life and eternal life, He is our light!"

Lucas was more than just afraid, but disturbed with some of the choices that he had made in his life as he asked Fr. Otto, "What about the choices in my life that Jesus would not approve of, what do I do now?"

Fr. Otto smiled at Lucas and replied, "When Jesus gave the Sermon on the Mount, he gave us something precious called the beatitudes and the first one is blessed are the poor in spirit, for the kingdom of heaven is theirs. This means blessed are those that understand their need for God. The beatitudes can lead us to the ecstasy of eternal life."

Before he finished his words, Fr. Otto walked closer to Lucas and placed his hand on his shoulder and said, "Whenever you're ready to confess your sins, I am ready to listen."

So many of us forget that God loves the sinner, just not the sin but through His Son we have forgiveness and a way to eternal life.

Lucas, before leaving Heaven's Gate, made a good confession.

The retreat was an enlightenment for the both of their lives as Gus and Lucas spent the return trip back to Quebec in solemn reflection. Each made an important decision. One left a personal article on the bridge before leaving while the other pondered a return visit.

Return to the real world meant more threats for Lucas and he wasn't sure how to handle the predicament for once Pandora's box is opened, the source of troubles never go away peacefully. The BHA was a strong force to contend with, but so was organized crime as a meeting between Lucas, Major General Smet and the powers-to-be came to order. The bureau expanded to all Canadian Provinces and became a threat-focused national security organization of some 8,500 personnel— a network of enforcement, kibitzers, informants, and spies to infiltrate and extract information vital to maintain national security. The spies were a network of men that were x-military or from the Mounted Police trained in covert operations to infiltrate, extract information and assassinate the enemy. The criminal organization became a yoke of bondage on society and needed to be eliminated like the skilled surgeon that cuts out the cancer. Realizing that the consequences could get ugly, Lucas encourages his dad to take a vacation in Maine and see the rest of the family.

"That's a fantastic suggestion, will you be coming with me son?" Gus is beckoning Lucas as he asks the question.

"No, Dad, I'm afraid I can't, too much business to take care of."

Lucas wanted to go and see his brother again but the sharp warning of acrimony from organized crime made him stay at the control of the helm of the BHA. The first letter received only said three words but those words penetrated through the skin to the bones. The first letter read, "Vengeance is forever!"

It was clearly an unending game of crime, bribery and death. And Lucas was afraid to drop the reins of control and allow organized crime to get the upper hand. A male nurse would accommodate his dad along with two undercover agents for his security. The train trip was monotonous and uncomfortable for Gus but the piece de resistance of seeing family and old friends made it all worthwhile. Gus perked up when he saw his son, grandson and old friend, Hjalmar waiting for him at the train depot. The next few days were extremely enjoyable for Gus spending time with his daughter-in-law, Olivia in the garden, a tour of the shipyard with his grandson, Adam and evenings playing a few hands of cribbage with his son and old friend, "H." In fact, it was "H" that told him, "It has been too long that the whole family has enjoyed a picnic at one of our favorite spots, Popham beach."

Arrangements were made, and it was good sitting there on the beach with his old friend enjoying a round of Drambuie's and admiring the beauty of the sea. Both men talked about the allurement of the sea and the beginning of their friendship as their minds floated back to a different time in the old country. As they admired the sunset and got ready to go back home, Hjalmar recalled the adage of, pink at night, sailor's delight and both men laughed for how true that had been for so many years. It wasn't easy pushing the wheelchair through the sand but for two old friends it indeed was an enjoyable time. So many fond memories but now much of it becoming a blur and Gus tried to remember back when he and Elsa came to Maine. Warm friendships, family love and kind words lift the spirits and some laughter as they watched the tide ebb and flow.

A shot rings out and echoes across the shore flinching everyone back to reality as Gus slumps over in his chair. An assassin's bullet, whose origin is not known, causes the security agents to scurry across the beach to no avail. How pointless, the absurdity of such a crime.

After weeks of endless investigation and no one to be found, the body was finally shipped home in a coffin. As the coffin was loaded on the train, Hjalmar stopped them long enough to say a short prayer. With tears in his eyes he placed both of his hands on the coffin and said this prayer:

"A gift from above, why do we deceive and take advantage of thee?
A precious gift to see & feel the love that should blossom in me.
The mirror of life; in His image creation came to be,
To nurture and build a beautiful paradise to see.
From the very beginning, the pluck of a delight; we tarnished,
His trust, His love, His very being; mankind did not garnish.
A heart and soul to believe, to perceive and give reverence back to thee,
Our short-comings make us stumble, our frailty to turn away and not see.
His gift to us, His son of majesty is a blessing for all,
His death to redeem us so that humankind shall not fall.
Agape Love such a beautiful, awe-inspiring gift to you and to me,

To pass through death, be eternally free and
give continual praise to thee.
Amen."

Svante accommodated the coffin back to Quebec so that
both brothers could bury their father. The day of the funeral
came and gone and the brothers confided in each other with
Svante learning of his brother's involvement with the
BHA. A promise was made by Lucas that he would get the
culprits that did this to their dad. An alarmed Svante cau-
tioning his brother that vengeance is mine says the lord!
Once Svante returned to Maine, then Lucas put into motion
a most cunning and devious plan.

A closed-door session between five of the most hard-
core, dauntless characters that could be assembled together
met in the shadows of the night at the BHA headquarters
with Lucas Bergstrom. Those in attendance were Major
General Smet, Staff Sergeant Mike McCuskey, explosive
ordnance disposal expert Carl Kushner and retired police
superintendent from Chicago, John McAvoy who was responsible for bringing down the six Sicilian brothers for
their crime spree. There were bloody Angelo, Mike, the
devil and Pete, Sam, Jim and Tony known as "the Gentleman" as they watched their henchmen twist a stiletto in
many of their foes' backs. Two of the gang's earliest gunmen were Sicilians Albert Anselmi and John Scalise found
in the bottom of the Chicago River with cement shoes and

police badges crammed down their throats. Hostile times call for hostile remedies and a Trojan horse was needed to execute the plan.

Organized crime was a thorn in the side for law enforcement agencies of both the United States and Canada. With the aid of retired police superintendent John McAvoy, both sides wanted to eliminate the crime family in Chicago. This hopefully would give a reprieve for Chicago of the rampant bribery of city officials and Canada another decade of peace, if that was at all possible; for, like rats, organized crime could multiply overnight. John McAvoy had an impressive repertoire of military service receiving the distinguished service cross and thirty-five years in the Chicago police enforcement doing everything from a beat cop to superintendent. That is until two of his sons that were also on the Chicago police force were gunned down by the mob. To maintain a secret, you didn't tell anyone anything in Chicago, hence the purpose for his appearing incognito in Canada.

Any story behind the Chicago mob should begin with the Porter House Hotel which is one about the affluent, mayhem and multiple vice in the city. Only the opulent could afford the $100,000.00 suites and there were several floors with lavish interior décor which beckoned both praise and mockery. The floor of the barber shop was tiled with silver dollars with a legend that proclaimed that there was a silver dollar for every bribe and murder committed by the mob. Located within the Loop of downtown Chicago, the Loop was the commercial hub and location of the main government offices for both the city and county. The Porter House was decorated with garnet-draped chandeliers, Louis Comfort Tiffany masterpieces and a breathtaking ceiling fresco by French painter Louis Pierre Rigal. The fresco was hailed by the columnist George Will as a wonderful protest of romance against the stark drabness of ordinary life. The hotel was conveniently located on Monroe Drive that connected all patrons to either Lake Shore Dr. or Lower Wacker Dr., the street dubbed for where the mob wacked many of their foes and dumped them into the Chicago River. The Porter House Hotel was home to the Chicago mob.

All the mob's clandestine meetings were held in the Golden Renaissance Room of the Porter House Hotel due to the double-steel wall construction. Double protection from bullets and eaves-dropping. Superintendent John McAvoy said to the group, "If there was ever a good place for a contained hit without any collateral damage; this is the place!"

"Fine," said MG Smet, "just how do we gain access and exit without being caught?"

Lucas broke into the conversation by saying, "That is why we have explosive ordnance disposal expert Carl Kushner and Staff Sergeant Mike McCuskey here. With McAvoy's logistics and their expertise, we are to execute the best hit in Chicago!"

Just then John McAvoy picked up the conversation with, "King pin, Luige Vilatorrio celebrates his birthday every year in the Golden Renaissance Room and in five months, he will be celebrating his seventieth birthday."

MG Smet added, "And with the help of both Carl and Mike with a big boom."

Laughter interrupts the conversation as Lucas says, "Let's have a round of drinks and toast our success to the big boom!"

Just then Lucas broke out the Drambuie, Glenlivet and some glasses. When drinks were finished, the meeting resumed with Lucas saying, "This plan was conceived some time ago, shortly after Gustavus was assassinated. I met John at one of the bureau meetings in the United States and we became good friends. Upon learning the death of his sons, we had mutual interest and wanted the same thing, retribution. Now we have a couple of Staff Sergeant McCuskey's men already positioned with jobs as delivery drivers for both Dressler's Bakery and the Red, White and Blue Apron Wine and Liquor Shop in Chicago. These shops make daily deliveries to the Porter House. Two things are essential here: one, familiarity with the hotel and two, easy access for our people."

There was a moment of silence while everyone begins to see the big picture.

"Now," Lucas resumed speaking, "With the expertise of Carl Kushner, explosives will be arranged in a large birthday cake that a couple of strippers are to jump out of for the old king pin."

Now Lucas gave his head a nod towards MG Smet to continue the talk, "Our Trojan horse will be the birthday cake but to pull this off, there must be two large birthday cakes. Everything is inspected before entering the room, hence two cakes, one for the strippers and one for the explosives and a switch will be made."

MG Smet paused before asking, "Any questions?"

Lucas picked up with the briefing where MG Smet left off by saying, "By the way, one of the men buried in the ski lodge avalanche was the son of Don Luige Vilatorrio. He came out of retirement to rebuild what was lost by the family syndicate."

The year that Henry Ford introduced the Model T car priced at a whopping $850 dollars, the unexpected assassination of twenty-two members of the Chicago mob took place at approximately 7:35 pm, August 20, 1908. There were enough explosives in the model cake to gut out the room and surrounding hallways.

The following decade were hollow years for Lucas, for the conspired assassination left him an empty person and it did not bring his father back. An estranged relationship worsened between him and Svante and without family or loved ones, life seems empty. He made a few more trips to Heaven's Gate and Otto's attempts at solace helped a little. But Fr. Otto was also experiencing difficult times as

Stefan's wife, Rosalind, died during their second child birth. Stefan was so devastated that he ignored their first son, Joshua, and Fr. Otto took in the boy at Heaven's Gate to rear him as an apprentice Oblate. Joshua is now eight years old and when he turns eighteen years old, if he so chooses can enter the brotherhood of the Oblates and study for the priesthood.

The winds of war disrupt life as we know it, for the first world war is just around the corner. The United States unsuccessfully tries to stay out of the war at first but with the sinking of the Lusitania and the loss of 1198 passengers, including 128 Americans; the threat of war with Germany could not be ignored. Kurt's sons are old enough to enlist in the Army to fight overseas and even though Indians were not liable to be drafted, they enlisted in large numbers eager to maintain the warrior traditions. An estimated 10,000 Indians served courageously during the first world war. After the war, President Warren G. Harding granted citizenship to all Native Americans who had served in World War I. Despite this, many Native Americans faced local resistance when they tried to vote and were discriminated against once again. The fate of the American Indian was still a thorn in Fr. Otto's side.

Subtleties in life can be the impetus to choose good over evil. Some say that getting off the path of life is the beginning of our faith and God is touching our heart to make the right choices. The trouble with humanity is simply this: too many people try to prevail without God's law.

For Lucas, his life was at a crossroads, much had happened and when he received another anonymous letter from the mob, his disillusionment grew worse. He went to the closet and removed a small suitcase to pack some clothes with the letter placed on top. His mind was racing as he proceeded to his office where he left a letter of resignation.

The two-day train ride to Heaven's Gate gave himself ample time to contemplate what he must do next.

Upon his arrival, Fr. Otto greeted Lucas and could sense his contempt as he led him to a cell for it is well past compline and silence is the observed rule.

Fr. Otto opened the door to the cell and placed the suitcase on the bed.

Lucas sat on the edge of the bed and places both of his hands over his face and muttered, "I just don't know what to do!" He then got up and removed the letter from his suitcase to give to Fr. Otto.

Fr. Otto read the short letter of three words, "Vendettas never stop!"

Sensing his trepidation, Fr. Otto realized that Lucas will not be able to sleep until he cleared his conscience.

Fr. Otto took out his stole and placed it over his shoulders, as Lucas knelt on the floor.

"Bless me, Father, for I have sinned," Lucas began to reveal the tale of the formation of the BHA, his sanction of hits, the loss of his father and possibly the loss of his soul.

After the confession, they talked for a while before Fr. Otto told Lucas, "Try to get some rest and meet me at the covered bridge at sunrise."

The next morning, Fr. Otto asked Lucas to remember what they had discussed last night. "Cross over the bridge, speak to God and he will give you rest."

At first as he followed the path there was a surge of anxiety that erupted within him, then as he read and contemplated the engraved stones, benevolence, and as he approached the bridge and looked up to see the words, "I am with you always," a sense of peace.

Lucas stepped out from the covered bridge, looked up towards the sun and then towards Fr. Otto, who was approaching him as an assassin's gunshot echoed from the edge of the woods.

Lucas fell to the ground as Fr. Otto rushed to his aid and cradled him in his arms. Bowing his head, Fr. Otto took his hand to sweep across the face of Lucas closing his eyelids.

Fr. Otto took upon himself to contact the family and ask permission of Lucas' brother to bury Lucas at Heaven's Gate. With his permission, preparations were made for the funeral.

The day of the funeral as the procession of Oblates carried the coffin from the church to the cemetery, there was Svante with his family, MG Smet and a few other guests. Unbeknown to anyone except for the Oblates, the empty coffin was lowered into the ground and a few words were read from the Bible. Lucas watched from afar from the bell-tower and had to fight the urge to run to his brother and let him know that he was still alive. But for the safety of their lives, it was better this way as he took the name of Br. James and allowed Lucas to exist no more. As the guests left Heaven's Gate, Br. James looked towards the sun that reminds us to do today what we may, for tomorrow is not a given and sunshine brings rays of hope for a new day.

The End